MICHAEL VAUGHN

SPECIAL DELIVERY

BOOK VI
OF THE
SAM PEPPERELL
PRIVATE INVESTIGATOR
SERIES

MICHAEL VAUGHN

BOOKS
BY
MICHAEL VAUGHN

(Romance)

Maid In Heaven

Sex In Malibu

(Drama)

Stroke Of Genius

Power Of The Order

(Mystery/Suspense)

Sam Pepperell Private Investigator Series

Faith And Legend

Who's Guilty

Call To Duty

Finders Keepers

It's Not What It Seems

Special Delivery

We All Need A Hero

(Paranormal Psycho Thriller)

The Hayden Keller Trilogy

Premonition

Resurrection

Walk Through Fire

For more about the author and upcoming books visit:

http://michaelvaughn.wix.com/books

Published in the United States by Powerhouse Press
Sam Pepperell Private Investigator
Special Delivery / Michael Vaughn

First Edition: 2014

ISBN-13: 9780692023631
ISBN-10: 0692023631

1. Boston private-eye 2. Red Sox World Series 3. Detective series
4. Murder investigation 5. Kidnapping case 6. Private investigator

Manufactured in the United States of America

Table Of Contents

Chapter 1

An Unexpected Curve

Sometimes life has its way of throwing you a curve you certainly never saw coming. In my line of work it was a common occurrence. With time, you learned to expect the unexpected. You learned from previous cases, and past experience, but you would think with time you would encounter it all. Eventually, everything would become old hat, almost mundane, and the surprise would no longer exist.

A woman would walk into your office and say, I need to know who killed my husband, whether it was my maid or my gardener, because the police suspect me, and I had nothing to do with his murder. You would then notice her look away as she finished her sentence leaving her butler unmentioned altogether, and there you would have your answer without ever leaving your office.

You'd say, I can tell you without a doubt it wasn't your maid or the gardener. It's quite obvious they're both involved with one another, but your husband wasn't the only one you were involved with, and that's how I know it was your butler. Nice and neat, short and sweet, you'd solve the case without ever pounding the pavement, but it never worked out like that, not in my fifteen years in this business.

Like any other profession, private investigating had its share of ups and downs, and what business you did have seemed to come in spurts. Whenever you weren't napping at your desk, you were in hopes the phone would ring, and you'd be working another case soon. If it was something a little out of the ordinary - that made it all the better.

Boston is known to be a tough town, and the trade which I chose to make myself a living was a tough business filled with its share of challenges, but the truth was I loved it cause it suited me well you could say. I should probably go ahead and let you know, my name is Sam Pepperell. Those that know me call me Pepper. I also happen to be the best damn private investigator in Boston since Willard Derkin pulled up stakes in this town, and this my story.

I had just finished working one of the most far reaching cases of my career. It started out as something close to nothing, and with a little digging it turned up a dead body along with a host of people that would've been more than willing to produce it. I wasn't hired to find the killer, just a package. I uncovered both because that's what I do.

On my way back to my office, I decided to take a different route strictly to do some case follow-up. I was curious about the end result of an unrelated case. Checking up on Mr. Melson and his wife, I was given an eyeful. It put a smile on my face though, I'll admit it. Pleasant surprises seldom present themselves to me. So, I've learned to appreciate them when they do show up.

The smile I mentioned didn't remain on my face for long. Taking the scenic route, mere blocks away from the Melson Estate, that grin faded quick as I entered a curve. Trouble had its way of finding me, and I never ran from it. Don't ask me why. That's just how God made me I guess. I was the perfect blend of stubborn and stupid to the point of believing I could really make a difference in this world. I was also staring at a woman in distress. I seemed to meet my share of them.

She was my next assignment, and she never had to hire me. She had my attention as soon as she ran right across the street in front of me. The truth was I damn near ran her over but Annette Jennings was a mother searching for her four year old boy. She was frantic as she screamed, "Jacob!" I stopped the car and got out. I was concerned for her safety since she was standing in traffic. That's when she turned to me shouting, "help me, please! I can't find my son!" I looked around, and had a bad feeling about this one.

Chapter 2

Facts Of The Matter

I seldom worked cases involving child abduction. This one would be number three if someone made off with her boy. I was hopeful that wasn't the case. Maybe he was just lost. The park was a big place after all. I yelled, "how old is he?" She told me his age, and my concern heightened though I tried not to show it. She was already in full panic mode. Standing there looking over the landscape of the arboretum she yelled out his name once again. Forced to gather the critical facts I immediately asked, "what's he wearing?"

"An orange jacket, a green shirt and blue jeans." She was no longer standing in the road, but I was blocking traffic. The woman behind me blew her horn. Mrs. Jennings uttered, "oh God. Jacob!"

I tried to keep her calm as I asked, "when and where was the last place you saw him?"

She struggled to catch her breath. "I don't know. A few minutes ago. He was standing right beside me. I was getting something out of the car."

"Where's your vehicle?" She pointed to her blue Ford Explorer parked fifty feet from where she was standing. That's when I heard the horn honk again. "Don't worry. I'm a detective. We'll find him." That's what I told her as she phoned her husband.

I was thinking positive at that point. What else could I do - tell her chances are she was never going to see her kid again? It was way too early for that call to be made. He could've easily just wondered off. That's what I was thinking as I approached the car behind me. I had to raise my voice because the woman refused to lower her window, but I informed her we had a missing child in the area. She cranked down the window enough to listen to the brief description I gave her. I wasn't bashful about asking for her help in finding the young boy.

She felt the need to ask, "are you a cop or something?"
"Detective."
"Am I in trouble for honking at you?"
"Not if you do your part to help us find this kid. What's your name?"
"Wanda Stark."
"Well Wanda, how about circling the perimeter of the park for me several times and keep an eye out for a four year old wearing an orange jacket. Can you do that for me?"
"Sure."

I had pulled out my notepad, and I was jotting down tag numbers. The guy behind Wanda had a kid in his vehicle, but he didn't match the description Annette Jennings had given me. "What's going on," he asked.
"Missing a four year old boy. You mind giving us a hand looking for him?"
"Yeah, no problem," he said.
"Orange jacket, green shirt, blue jeans, his name is Jacob." This guy cared enough to park his car, and help search the tree preserve on foot with his own son. He appeared to be about nine or ten."

I had hastily written down a dozen tag numbers of cars in the general area. Two minutes had passed since I rolled up on the scene. Enlisting the help of five individuals to fan out and search for Jacob, I interviewed his mother. "Did you see anyone nearby right before your son went missing?"
"No."

"Did you hear anything, a voice, the sound of a vehicle pull up, a car door shut?"

"No. I mean I don't know. There was traffic. Some guy was walking his dog, but he was on the other side of the street. Please, you've got to help me find my son."

She was desperate. I didn't bother asking questions about the guy with the dog or vehicles she noticed missing. I wanted to, but I refrained. She needed peace of mind, something she wouldn't have until her son was returned to her - even I knew that.

I must have been feeling heroic at that point, but it's no excuse. I broke rule number three which is don't make promises to anyone. Willard was a stickler for adhering to that one, and I had a tendency to bend it on occasion. This was one of them. "I will find your son," I told her. "You wait right here for your husband, and I'll bring him back to you." Jacob had been missing roughly seven minutes at that point. Four minutes later, I found his orange jacket lying on the ground behind a tree a hundred yards from where I first met his mother. That wasn't a good sign.

There was no doubt in my mind someone had taken Jacob Jennings. Things race through your mind at that point like, what are you going to say to his mother, but all that mattered was - what was my next move. It didn't take me thirty seconds to form a damn plan. It was bold, edgy and attention grabbing, but that's what it was going to take to get Jacob Jennings back in the arms of his mom. I'm sure it didn't follow standard protocol, and part of it was probably illegal, but I had little doubt it wouldn't work if promptly executed. That's what mattered when you got down to it. I didn't give a damn about consequences. I could deal with those later. Getting the kid back alive as soon as possible was my primary focus, and I was about to break a few rules to accomplish just that.

I had made a promise to Annette Jennings whose name I didn't even know at that point, but I was determined to deliver on that promise no matter what it took. The clock was ticking, and I had my work cut out for me. Instantly, it became the most important case in my life. Maybe that's because a kid was involved, or maybe it was rule number three, combined with a mother's love for her missing child which made this one special, but the case changed my life. I'll go right ahead and tell you that now. If anyone could find Jacob Jennings it was me.

Chapter 3

Unlikely Counterparts

My initial impulse was to break down, and do it. It's a given doing the right thing is seldom ever easy in a case like this but Lana made things more complicated. Make the damn call Pepper, that's what I told myself. The stubborn side of me put up its defense, but it was no match for my tactical mind. Lana Osborne was a local reporter. She was a hellcat in person, out on the street, and a tigress in the sack, but that's another story I won't delve too deep into. Some things which take place between the sheets should remain personal. It's fair to say we knew one another well.

She liked to take cheap-shots at me when given the chance, and anything she could do to make my life miserable she did it with pleasure. She also loved me once, I'm convinced of it. Although, you couldn't tell it now. I never liked talking to her, and more times than not, I avoided her calls, but now I found myself needing a favor. Pulling out my cell phone, I dialed her number. Even though I hadn't done so in quite some time, I knew it by heart.

She knew it was me as soon as she picked up. I could tell by the sound of her hostile voice when she said, "what the hell do you want?" That was her way of saying hello, to me anyway. Did I mention we were once married? It was a turbulent time in my life filled with rationed sex and lots of demands mostly made by her whenever she could catch me standing still for a spilt-second.

It pained me to say it, but I did. "I need your help." Hearing her rapidly exhale through her nose, the rush of air said as much as her words did, maybe more. "What's new?" She made it sound as though it were a common occurrence when I was the one that consistently saved her ass from the fire. All she had to say is, I need you Sam.

There were countless times I rushed to her aid on request, and I worked many a free case for her just because she was my ex. Standing there in Arnold Arboretum with an orange parka in my hand that would only fit a preschooler, I didn't have time to remind her of that. If I did, she would've just hung up leaving me with no help at all. As punishment, she would have blocked my calls, and forced me to find some other way to recover Jacob for his mother.

The greatest advantage I had was knowing exactly how her mind worked. Most men can't say that about many women, but I knew her most deep-seated desires. That was the key to working Lana. You had to work her, or she'd end up working you. If I gave her what she wanted though, she would do what I asked as long as it behooved her in the end. All I had to do to get her to play ball was throw her a bone.

You're probably saying that's no way to talk about her Pepper. She's your ex-wife not a dog. Well, when it came to landing a big story she'd do anything to get it. Once she had hold of it, she wouldn't let go until she milked it for everything it was worth, and chewed it to pieces just like a damn dog with a bone. She could also be a bitch when warranted, and I say that with a degree of respect.

The profession which she chose, and loved was a tough one as well, but it suited her to a tee. She looked damn good on camera doing it, and sometimes I would tell her that.

Lana wore compliments well. The passion we both shared for what we did made us better at it. The similarities between us ended there though. Lana and I were polar opposites in many ways, but we both uncovered stories. She broadcasted hers to the world, and I passed mine on to the people that paid me to do the needed investigative work.

When it came to dealing with me, she played by a special set of rules, anything was fair, and she's the last person I'd ever call if I ended up in a holding cell. That being the case, I was going to tell her what I needed her to hear, embellish things a little, and point out the benefits of aggressive reporting in a case like this. Being at the head of this lead story would later be touted as instrumental in finding the boy. Her zeal for sensational reporting told me I wouldn't have to twist her arm to get her to spearhead this one.

Investigative journalism was a competitive field if you wished to do well in it for the long-term. She had bigger dreams though. That was one of the many reasons she was no longer with me. Maybe, some would say I couldn't give her all she hoped for. In all honestly, no man could. That's why she collected husbands like passports gather stamps. Success had its' way of attaching itself to her though, I suppose. Look at me.

She liked to call it trading up. I liked to call her flaky, and fickle, but never to her face, not when I needed something. The other thing I can tell you about her is she never forgot anything. Hence, she was now on marriage number three working her way up the financial rungs toward something better. One day it wouldn't surprise me to find her seated inside the Governor's mansion no longer holding a microphone. All that aside, no matter who she married, or where life took her, she would always call me number one.

Compelling her to do what I wanted was as simple as saying, "I've got a story for you."

"What is it this time, cat up a tree or lost dog?" She was the queen of sarcastic cheap-shots.

"Try missing four year old boy taken from Arnold Arboretum less than fifteen minutes ago."

Instantly, she dropped what she had in her hand. I could hear her scurrying to get something to write with. "Tell me what you know."

"The boy's name is Jacob. He was wearing an orange jacket at the time of the abduction, but now he no longer is. The mother said he was wearing a green shirt, and blue jeans."

"You actually spoke with her?"

"Promised I'd do what it took to get her boy back."

"You know you shouldn't have done that. Rule number three remember."

She knew the rules as well as I did, maybe better, but she was a stickler for rules. She'd have trouble breaking them if her life depended on it. I, on the other hand, ran rough shot over them half the time, not that I'm proud of that. I felt guilty whenever I did it. It was like I was somehow cheating on Willard, my conscience verses his rules to play by. He was my mentor in case you didn't know. Lana on the other hand had no conscience. She was just a control freak. We had been divorced well over a decade, and she was still telling me what to do.

Right away she asked, "how do you plan on getting him back?"

"I'm holding evidence with the kidnapper's DNA on it, and as soon as I get off the phone with you, I have to call one of my contacts at the Boston P.D. Just thought I'd go ahead and give you a heads-up before every reporter in town hears the chatter over police radios."

"You did that for me?"

She was skeptically touched by it when she questioned me, and I knew better than to outright lie to her. Always bleed a little truth into an untruth, and you can usually sell it to those who know you best. "I did it for Jacob, and his mom as well as you."

"How did you become involved with the case? Did she phone you?"

"She ran across the street in search of her son, when I discovered he was missing."

"I want to speak with the mother. What's her name?" Her voice sounded eager, and that meant she was willing to bend over backwards.

"I'll give you the details when you get here."

"I'm going to get a camera crew over there right now. What's your exact location?"

"Arborway southwest of Saint Rose Street."

"Don't let her speak to anyone other than police. I want this exclusive. You got it?"

"Well you can have it if you air this immediately."

"What do you want me to do, interrupt regular scheduled programming?"

"That's what gets people's attention isn't it."

"Yeah, you're right about that." Her mind was racing at that point envisioning the shock factor and drama of the story she would be telling. She knew it could hit CNN. That was the perfect time for me to tell her what to do.

"Listen. You be sure to mention a detective is working the case, and an item tying the kidnapper to the crime scene has already been recovered."

"Okay anything else?"

"Yeah, you can tell them a fund has been set-up offering a substantial reward to anyone providing critical information which helps in finding Jacob, and be on the look-out for anyone with a boy matching his description."

"Okay, and I get the interview with the mother."

"You always get what you want."

"That's why I married you Sam." That was as affectionate as either of us got, except for when she was between husbands. Right now, what mattered was pressuring the person that held the boy into letting him go. The way you do that is turn up the heat quick to the point they believe keeping the kid puts them in certain danger of being apprehended. When I was done, that abductor was going to buy into the fact a statewide dragnet was underway led by the feds no less.

I hung up on Lana right as she did on me. Then before dialing police I phoned Graham, the best damn con man to ever take up the trade. He knew it was me before he ever answered, "what's up Pepper?" He screened every call without fail for good reason, and seeing my name on his caller ID, next thing out of his mouth was, "give me the angle."

"I'm trying to find a missing boy age four, and you're the FBI agent."

"I like it."

"Figured you would. You're probably going to want to use a burn phone for this one."

"You wouldn't believe it, but it just so happens I've got one. Any particular name you need me to use?"

"That's up to you, you're the professional."

I told him what to say, and who to call. Giving him the numbers to dial I instructed him, "make it short and sweet and don't test boundaries, a kid's life is at stake."

"Alright, understood."

Chapter 4

Interviewing The Jennings

Jacob had been missing twenty minutes when his father arrived. A minute later, his mother turned to notice me carrying his jacket as I walked toward her. That's when she broke down, and her husband's heart sank. Fortunately, he was there to hold her. I remember my first words to him when he asked, "where'd you find that?"

"About four hundred feet in that direction. Police have been notified. There's also a news reporter wanting to get this story on television in order to inform the public your son is missing." I mentioned nothing about kidnapping. I didn't have to. He and his wife were smart enough to figure that out.

"He couldn't have gotten that far on his own, and he wouldn't have taken off his jacket."

"I know."

"You said you would find him. So, stop standing here."

She was livid. I couldn't blame her for lashing out at me. I was nobody in her world, all that mattered was her kid. I understood that. I made the effort to tell them, "I will find him with the help of everyone in Boston. Right now, it's imperative we get the word out in case anyone spots him. I'm sorry I didn't catch your name."

"Stephen Jennings."

"Well, just give the reporter a clear description of your boy, and you will get him back." Her face was filled with tears. She tried to explain she only took her eyes off of him for a minute. I said nothing but the thought which ran through my mind was *that's all it takes lady.*

As soon as Lana came on the scene, she informed me the feds were already looking into the case. That kind of made the Jennings' feel better given the circumstances. I knew the feds weren't working the case yet though. Graham made that call to Lana at my request. I should have never given him so much leeway though.

Graham had to go and use the name Agent Cringle. He was no saint either. What made him decide to use Santa Clause's last name as an alias I'll never know, probably cause he knew he could get away with it over the phone. Fortunately, Lana never doubted him for a second. I could have kicked his ass for pulling that stunt, but he could introduce himself as Johnny Carson, and you'd be looking for a performance from Doc Severinsen.

Lana may not have known con men that impersonate federal agents can't resist using names of obvious fictional characters, but she knew how to pitch the story, and get it in front of everyone. I did my best to stay off camera. She laid everything out just like I encouraged her to, and at that point, I knew what was happening down at the main precinct. Cops which had been sitting on their asses were now scratching their heads questioning who was working the case. The police had been notified, but that made word spread ten times faster.

It would only be a matter of time before the added 911 calls would inevitably overload the system until a special number was given to the public so they could call about the non-existent reward money. When Lana pressed me about the hotline number, I simply said, "it hasn't been set up yet. Just dial 911."

Off camera after the live broadcast, she cornered me saying, "there's no reward money is there?"

"Sure there is."

"Really, how much?" I dug in my front pocket pulling out my money clip, and some change. I was holding forty-two dollars and thirty-eight cent. That's when she started cursing. "Damn it, Sam! Do you have any idea what you just made me do?" Truth was she didn't really have any idea how many lies she told during that broadcast, and I wasn't about to tally them up for her.

"You might want to keep your voice down."

"There's something else you're not telling me isn't there."

"I've gotta go. Look you did great, but I have to find this kid."

"You're not getting away that easy." Her phone rang, and she stepped away from me to answer it. The police chief was on the other end of the line, and he wanted details she had. Who was her FBI contact? That must have been one of the first questions. I heard her offer up Agent Cringle's name. Way to go Graham. I was slowly putting distance between myself, and her, but I didn't get far. In the process of handing over evidence to one of the officers that had rolled up on the scene I heard her order me, "Sam get over here. Someone important wants to talk to you. Make it quick because I have questions for him."

I stuck to facts that were important to the case. Mention of FBI agents, and reward money never came up in the one minute I spent on the phone with him. He wanted my direct number though. So, I gave it to him. That's when I handed the phone back to Lana. I'd let them battle each other over information. I knew who would win that one. Initially, I figured the person holding the kid would drop him as if he were a hot potato, or try to cash him in for reward money, depending on how stupid they were. Apparently, I was wrong.

Chapter 5

Questionable Outcome

Hours had past, and the real FBI now expressed interest in where Jacob Jennings was. I played dumb about a lot of things cause that's what I do best at times. I knew it was only a matter of time before I was called into the police station to answer some questions. When the case first came about, and I initiated the investigation, most were on my side. Now that hours had past, and the boy wasn't returned to his family, questions about proper procedure cropped up. I was the one people pointed to.

I remember sitting inside the office belonging to the chief of police. The invitation I received from him to be there was less than cordial. We were both waiting on one call, the call which said Jacob Jennings had been found alive and well, but in the meantime he was chewing me out. The ironic part was I didn't even work for the guy, but given the circumstances, I was starting to feel it was warranted. I couldn't blame him really. He was feeling pressure from the Boston Police Commissioner, and the FBI had their feathers ruffled along with everyone else.

I kept in mind something Willard once said, "tension builds before the storm. You've got to breathe out, and breathe in – keep doing that and before you know it, it'll be over." Willard also said, "what's left is the aftermath - take it as it comes." I didn't share those words with anyone, I just ran them through my mind as I waited, hoping for the best.

What I heard from the chief was, "you shouldn't have gotten the media involved in this the way you did. You should have come to us first, put it in the hands of real professionals." I tried to argue my case. I conducted a search, and made the necessary calls.

All I could offer in defense of my actions was, "whoever has the kid can't hold onto him at this point. They'll have to let him go." That last statement wasn't the only option for the kidnapper, but it was the only one I would entertain.

It was now dark outside. The longest hour of my life passed as I sat in that seat staring at his phone. Dread seemed to fill the room but when it did ring, we both had questionable hope. When it didn't, we stared at each other. He was now aware of my previous arrest record, and he made sure I knew it. He leaned forward placing his elbows on his desk as he spoke. "So, you're the guy that vandalized Boston Common a few months back." He clasped his hands together, and pulled them to his chin waiting for my response.

"I was in the process of preventing a stalker from having his way with his prey. I saved a woman's life."

"Yeah, I read your statement in the report. You don't seem to have the best of luck in parks do you?" I didn't respond to that, we just continued waiting. He didn't want to say it, but he had to. "What are you going to do if you're wrong?"

"Quit trying to help people I guess."

"Yeah." That's when his phone rang for a third time. It wasn't the police commissioner or some random officer. Whoever he was talking to informed him they had the kid in their charge.

The kidnapper had waited til dark to drop Jacob off at the mall. The police chief looked at me saying, "looks like you're still in business." Inside, I was elated, outside I remained calm while he gave specific orders to police on the scene. "I want every security camera in the area checked, and I want statements from any witnesses seeing who dropped him off." Reflecting back on the words a hardened old private investigator once shared with me I suppressed a fast emerging smile at that point, Willard was right.

I listened to him instruct the officers to gather any tangible evidence. Then he said, "I want the child brought here immediately, his parents are waiting for him." Hearing that I stood from the hot-seat I occupied ready to exit his office before he got off the phone. All of the crap he received from the police commissioner didn't really matter at that point. Jacob had been recovered successfully, and that looked good for Boston P.D. He gruffly barked, "hold it," when I went to turn the knob on his door to leave. Last words he growled at me were, "good work on helping find the kid." I didn't say anything. I was just ready to get the hell out of there.

There would be plenty of disgruntled tipsters that sought financial compensation from a reward fund which didn't exist. Best I could offer them was a thank you for their help, and nothing more other than a paid for hotdog from Joe's cart. Something is better than nothing right. That's what went through my mind as most celebrated. I wasn't the one that actually delivered Jacob to his parents, but I remained there at the station long enough to see him reunited with his mother. I said nothing to him, just put eyes on him. A female office was actually the one to hand him over to his parents, and she, it seemed, had built quite the rapport with him.

My impression was Jacob probably never met a stranger.

Now he had even more people that wanted to talk to him like the sketch artist. He was inquisitive, and proud of his age. That's all I can tell you about him really. The press was on the steps waiting for the Jennings' to leave. There were details to tend to in the case though before that could happen.

Tyler Probst was a forensic artist. He sketched people's faces based on someone else's recollections, and descriptive words. He belonged somewhere else other than a police precinct, but they were fortunate to have him. He had just finished listening to Jacob describe the man that dropped him off at the mall. Four year olds don't give great descriptions by the way. So, I didn't expect much to come from that sketch. Tyler got three statements out of Jacob. "He was big like my dad. His hair was like mine, but he didn't have much. Oh, and he had a dog." He couldn't really describe the color van he was in. It was a dark color though.

Jacob didn't care at that point. He didn't understand what the big fuss was about. He was unharmed, and back with his parents. In his mind he had an adventure. He found his parents, saw policemen, and got to pet a dog. Those were the highlights for him. For his mother, the highlight was holding him again. His father wrapped his arms around them both as he looked in my direction. He was at a loss for words, but that's okay nothing had to be said at that point. I made it easy on him saying, "all in a day's work. You be sure and tell that reporter outside, that Boston P.D. got your boy back."

Annette Jennings looked over at me saying, "thank you so much."
I just nodded stating, "a promise is a promise." As I turned

to walk away, Tyler stopped me. He had reached for my arm when I walked by his chair. Making the oddest request, he asked me to stand still just for a moment. He put his pencil to his sketch pad and quickly went to work scratching out a drawing. The Jennings were already pictured on it when I turned to face him.

I felt stupid standing there, but what he handed me two minutes later made it worth the wait. He tore the drawing out of the sketch pad, and handed it to me saying, "this is for you, for a job well done." The guy was gifted. I was given something unique that meant something crafted by his hand. I would never forget that case either. One day that drawing might even make my office wall I thought, all it would take is a frame, and a little spare time to put it there.

Tyler Probst received a handshake in return for his ability to capture the moment. He had several other drawings of the man believed to have kidnapped Jacob. They were similar in appearance for the most part. Looking at them, I had no doubt, given time, he would be brought in for questioning and placed in a line up. Tyler credited me with generating those eyewitnesses. I preferred not to think about that though. Most of those people would surely be looking to get paid by someone.

With the picture in hand it was time to make my exit. I had overstayed my welcome as soon as I entered the building. My best chance of making it out of there without the cameras flashing in my face, was to skip-out right behind Mr. and Mrs. Jennings using them, and their son as a shield. Turning to face them I asked, "are you guys ready for this?"
Stephen Jennings twisted his head rather quick proclaiming, "we won't forget you."
"After you then."

They had no idea how quick I planned on exiting stage left, but it really didn't matter. The press wanted to hear from them, and Lana would be the one they talked directly to. Moving down the steps, I heard numerous voices shouting questions at them. Lana had taken control of the interview by the time I reached the sidewalk. Opening the door to my car, I heard her ask, "is there anyone you'd like to thank?"

Annette Jennings and her husband were overwhelmed when they spoke, but they did it far better than the president. They included everyone in their passionate praise from the Boston Police Department, and all of its members to the concerted efforts of the media in the case. The FBI even received an honorable mention.

I listened to every word as I climbed into my '64 Fairlane. They made certain to thank the great people of Boston as well. "Without everyone working together, we wouldn't even want to think what the outcome would be." That was the final quote I heard from them, not one mention of me, and I appreciated that.

Driving away, I felt I had done a good thing, made the world a better place for once, and although it wasn't here yet, I could feel tomorrow was a new day. I, for one, was ready for it.

Chapter 6

Case Aftermath

The case ended happily. Seldom did events unfold in such a way, and that made for a glorious day in the city of Boston. On the surface I knew one thing – the Jacob Jennings case would allow me the weather the rough days in this business for years to come. It would reinforce my resolve to keep trying to help people. "You hold onto the wins." That's what Willard used to say. Lana reminded me of that when she met me at my office the next day asking if I saw the Jennings interview she did? She knew the answer to that question before she asked it. "I've got better things to do than sit around and watch TV," I groaned.

"You were never mentioned." I said nothing. I knew she was fishing for a response of some sort. "Just how you like it, I suppose." I remained silent as I reached down opening my center desk drawer. Pulling out the drawing Tyler had crafted for me I laid it on my desk. She stared down at it saying, "I think I know that guy."

"At least I got something out of it."

"You plan on keeping it in that desk of yours your whole life?"

"Hey, I just received it last night."

"That's no excuse. Next time I come in here it better be on the wall."

"Who says there's a next time?"

"There always is with you Sam," and with that she turned and headed for the door. "Congratulations on saving that boy's life with my help of course."

"Report it any way you want, just leave my name out of it."

"Always do, don't I." Whatever she said after that, I couldn't make out. It wasn't worth hearing anyway, I'm sure of it.

The days which followed were unpleasant for me. The repercussions were coming though my phone line. I made up my mind that was the last kid case I was getting involved with. Jacob Jennings was a curious little boy that had gotten me in trouble but he was still alive. Maybe some of it was my own doing, but it was only to help him. The kid was safe that's what mattered, but try telling that to concerned citizens looking for a payday of some sort. I heard a lot of F/Us on my recorder. What I discovered, based on the messages left on my answering machine, is these people were highly pissed off. Make no mistake about it, I archived those numbers just in case someone took a pot shot at me. Lana kept my name quiet, but someone spoke it to the newspaper. Teddy had to show me, of course. "I knew you had something to do with this one." He had seen some camera footage of me slinking down the steps of the police precinct where the Jennings family was interviewed. Teddy didn't miss anything. He tore out the article claiming he was going to save it for me.

"I don't want it," I told him.

"You will someday," he said. "Maybe when you screw your head on straight, until then I'll keep up with it." I tried to snatch it from his hand, but Teddy was fast. He shined shoes for a living, and he had been grabbing money out of people's hands since he was seven. So, snatching something out of his hand was next to impossible. That's when he dubbed me the kid detective. He knew I didn't like it. That's why he egged me on about it. I made one thing clear to him though, that was going to be the last time I took a case involving a kid. His response was, "we'll see about that."

Chapter 7

Business And Baseball

The weeks which passed after the case of the missing kid gave me the break I needed. Business had slowed, my bills were at bay, and baseball was in full swing. The Sox were doing well I might add, but you know what happens when everything goes right. Eventually, it goes wrong. That's what Willard always assured me of. He was an old sports fan like me. So, it's only natural that he liked to refer to it as the curveball. "You never know when it's coming, but sooner or later it will reach the plate, I guarantee you that."

After the Jennings case, I didn't doubt those words so much. I knew there would be another curveball headed for me, I just had no idea it would show up so soon. So, I might as well tell you the story which followed, and how a seasoned detective received the surprise of his life in the form of a special delivery. It was a package that would change my world, turn it upside down even. It would leave me asking what's next for a long time to come, but in the end in some odd way it made me a better man in the process, as if that were possible, or so I'd like to think. Again, I'm jumping the gun a little by saying that at this point. Every story has a beginning. So, it's best to start there I suppose.

The phone rang just as the parcel service guy walked into my office. I answered it, "Sam Pepperell Detective Agency. This is Pepper. How can I help you?" The guy handed me his clipboard pointing to a blank line on one of the pages for me to sign. He said something about a special delivery while I listened to a distraught woman on the other end of the line. It was the usual, she suspected her husband of having an affair with another woman, and she started crying as she told me all her concerns.

Just so you have a clue as to what I hear in this line of work, I'll run part of the conversation by you. She started off with, "Dennis hired a new secretary just last month, and his work schedule changed almost immediately. First, it started with late nights, and now he supposedly has to work weekends. I just know something's going on, and I don't know what to do about it. I mean what would you do?"

Hastily reaching for a pen, I quickly made my mark in the appropriate spot for the parcel guy as I tried to reply with, "well, I'd," but that's all I could get out. She abruptly cut me off. Two words uttered, one of them a contraction in the first minute of the conversation that was pretty good. Now, it was time for her to get hysterical. I glanced at my watch timing her as I handed the clipboard back to the delivery guy.

He then informed me, "your package is sitting on the sofa by your door in the other room."
I just waved my hand at him saying, "thanks, I'll take care of it."

He quickly turned heading for the door, and I turned my attention back to Mrs. Burke when she questioned if I was listening to her. A simple, "yes ma'am" was all that left my lips, and she was off, and running once again.

The delivery man sounded as if he said something when he walked into the other room, but I couldn't make it out over Mrs. Burkes tearful yammering. "You know, I've given him the best years of my life, and I can't believe he's screwing around on me with that little tart."

I chimed in with, "well maybe," but that was as far as I got. Mrs. Burke had a little drama queen embedded deep within her personality, and she was ready to let it out.

"She's practically young enough to be his daughter, and she's not fooling anyone with that hair. She's definitely not a real blonde, that's all I'm saying. She dresses like a street walker too, you know in those short skirts, and low cut tops."

Honestly, Mrs. Burke made her sound like my kind of girl, although, I didn't dare admit it. Apparently, the young woman fell into that category for Mr. Burke as well, according to his wife. Openly voicing her thoughts, she continued her rambling questioning choices she had made in her life. "What can I say? My mother warned me. She never liked Dennis to start with. She always said I should have married Cliff Barksdale instead. She was probably right. I mean, he does own his own accounting firm."

From her brief remarks, I gathered she valued money. How much of it she had, I couldn't be sure. She spoke as though she was no stranger to it, but she was a soon to be client, there was no question there. Her voice may have seemed shaken, but she was determined. I had heard it all before. Mr. Burke had better hope he was truly being overworked, and his wife was overly paranoid, otherwise he was in for it.

I tried to interject, "look, Mrs. Burke." You guessed it, she cut me off again, but she was finally winding down. She was now at the stage where she was just going to go for the throat. Women were like that, they either remained fretful and depressed by the idea they were being cheated on, or they became vicious.

Men tended to handle things differently. They were either depressed, and remorseful, or overly agitated and highly suspicious. Often they were enraged by the thought of their wife running around on them, but most of those guys took matters into their own hands. Few of them had a need for a private investigator unless they had plenty of money to protect in a divorce proceeding, but this was Mrs. Burke we're talking about now, isn't it.

The last thing she said was, "I want you to find out exactly what he's doing, and if he is getting his toast buttered somewhere else, I want proof, I mean pictures and lots of them. Cause so help me God, I am going to get the most expensive damn divorce attorney in this town, and I'm going to take him for everything he's got."

Finally it was my turn to speak, "well Mrs. Burke, let's hope it doesn't come to that, but I can take your case, and get to the bottom of it fairly quick, that I am certain." At that moment, I looked up from my desk to see a pair of emerald green eyes staring right at me. They belonged to a little girl I had never seen before. She appeared to be about seven or so. Only problem was I didn't see anyone with her.

I've handled my share of off the wall cases, but kids without parents were not my specialty. I moved my head looking into the other room expecting her mother to be close by, but I couldn't see anyone from where I was sitting. I placed my hand over the phone as I continued holding it to my ear. That's when I asked, "where's your mom?"

A saddened looked surfaced on the girl's face, but she said nothing. I knew something was wrong, but I had no idea what I had gotten myself into this time. "Let me get your number Mrs. Burke, and I'll call you right back." I finished scribbling down the number on my notepad, and I hung up the phone. Then I offered the young girl a seat in the chair on the other side of my desk, and I asked what her name was.

She replied, "Kelsey. Is your name really Pepper?"

"Well, that's what they call me. How can I help you, Miss Kelsey?"

"You don't have to call me Miss Kelsey, I'm only a kid."

"Really," I replied.

She must have found the expression on my face somewhat amusing since she giggled a little at that point. I was quite accustomed to conferring with clients seated in that chair, but kids were not my strong suit, not by a long shot. Things being what they were, my curiosity got the best of me, and I asked her another question. "Well what are you doing in my office?"

She looked around the room saying, "sitting in your chair. Is all this stuff yours?"

I looked around at the stacks of papers and file folders throughout my office. There was hardly anywhere you could look and not find them. The table wedged in between my filing cabinets was completely covered by the mess, and several boxes underneath it were filled to capacity with surveillance equipment and other junk.

Looking up at the shelf on the wall adjacent to her which was filled with a hodgepodge of stuff, most of it personal, I answered her. "Yeah, the whole kitten-ka-boodle." My eyes scanned over the top of my desk, and they landed on my Wade Boggs signed baseball next to my Boston Celtics coffee mug.

Instinctively, I picked up the ball and casually tossed it in air catching it with my other hand as I said, "I guess what I meant to say is why are you in my office."

"I'm your special delivery, silly. You're supposed to take me to meet my aunt."

"Oh, you've gotta be kidding me."

Chapter 8

My New Sidekick

At that very moment, I knew someone must have been playing a practical joke on me. At least, that's what I hoped. The kid looked as though she was serious. I stuck my head in the other room to see if anyone was there. I even opened the door looking outside my office. The hallway was empty. Turning to look back over my shoulder at the chair where the little girl was sitting, to my surprise, she was no longer in it.

My Wade Boggs signed baseball hit the floor when I walked back into my office. Utterly perplexed, I stood there looking at her sitting behind my desk. She had made herself quite comfortable, swiveling back and forth in my chair. That's when she said, "hello. How can I help you?" I thought you can start by getting out of my chair, but I said nothing. I didn't have to, she was like Mrs. Burke - she never shut up. She continued with, "take a seat, please. Forgive me for the mess. The maid is off today, but someone really needs to clean this place up." It was like she had taken over the place. She hadn't been inside my office five minutes when she started fidgeting and fumbling through papers on my desk attempting to place them all in one neat pile.

I know I kind of went a little nuts when I raised my voice a smidge clearly instructing her, "no, don't do that! I have everything right where I want it! Trust me, I have a very unique filing system, and I know where everything in this room is. So, keep your hands off of it. Okay?"

That happy look on her face slowly went away as she stared up at me. Alright, I went a little overboard, I admit it. I'm not proud of it, but like I said, I'm not good with kids. That's not to say I don't like them cause that's not the case at all. I just like them from a distance. I'm sure some of you know what I mean, but with that said, I didn't know what was going on.

All I did know was I just had the tables turned on me by a seven year old, and admittedly, she wasn't bad for seven, but I'm no babysitter. Parenthood was just never in the cards for me, but that's alright. Not all of us are cut out for raising kids, certainly not an old rough around the edges P.I. like me.

She looked a bit frightened, maybe on the verge of tears. I didn't need that on top of everything else. Attempting to set her at ease I said, "look if you want to straighten something you can work with that pile of papers over there, but that's the only ones you touch. Got it?"
She nodded her head smiling, and she repeated what I said, "got it." She quickly walked over to the pile of papers I pointed to as I took my rightful place behind my desk, and reached for my rolodex. Wasting no time, I began to grill her. "What's your aunt's name?"

She meticulously placed each individual piece of paper in the pile in a nice neat stack one on top of another as she slowly pronounced her aunt's name dragging every letter out to form, "Rhea."

She was quite entertaining to watch actually, but I had an aunt to find, and lucky for me her name was a bit out of the norm. That would certainly make her easier to locate, but one thing's for certain, I had never spoken to anyone about this special delivery. My guess was someone figured they could dump the girl off with me, and I'd do all the work to locate the girl's guardian for free just to get rid of her. Well, they were probably right. "You got a last name kid?"

"Yeah."

"Well what is it?"

"Fallon."

That name sounded familiar. It didn't take long to place it either, but chances of her being related to the guy I was thinking of were slim to none. Still, one must ask the question. "You're not related to Eddie Fallon are you?"

"Yeah, he's my uncle. You know him?"

"Yeah, I'm afraid so."

Chapter 9

Lewisburg Pen

Reaching Eddie by phone was extremely difficult unless you were his attorney, but I knew where I could find him. He wasn't going anywhere for a long time. You see Eddie Fallon was a three time loser doing hard time in the federal penitentiary down in Lewisburg, Pennsylvania. That place was no country club. I had visited it myself. The other thing I can tell you about Eddie is he was the worst criminal in the world, not worst as in he was a bad guy you'd never hope to meet in a dark alley, but bad as in just plain bad at not getting caught.

Eddie should have chosen another profession. He had all the skills of an artist, but no luck whatsoever, none worth having anyway. He was a paper man by trade, for those unfamiliar with the term, Eddie drafted and forged legal papers. He was gifted at it. I'd have to say the best in the business when it came to falsifying documents and forging signatures. Eddie could sign anyone's name to anything, and you'd believe it was real.

Come to think of it, he's the one that gave me the Wade Boggs signed baseball. Well, there's no real need to get that thing authenticated now, is there. I'm pretty sure we all know where that signature came from. I preferred to think, at the time he gave it to me, that he came by it honest prior to his incarceration, but this was Eddie Fallon we're talking about. He began making fake IDs at the age of eleven, and he never stopped. Like they say, when you find something you're good at, stick with it. In Eddie's case they should have added, and don't get caught.

It was a little over three years ago when I first met him. He was on the other side of the protective glass dressed in orange when he asked for my help. Normally, I didn't make trips out of state to visit convicted felons still serving out their sentences, but it was his letters that brought me to see him in person. He was convincing on paper - what can I tell you. I needed the money, and he promised to pay me three grand just to track down someone he knew. It sounded easy enough.

The man he was after left him holding a lot of bad plastic, and incriminating paper, everything the Feds needed to put Eddie away for a long time. They don't take kindly to bank fraud. In my opinion, from what I saw, this guy planned it that way right from the start. He used Eddie like an old dust mop, mainly to do all the dirty work in setting up hundreds of accounts, then when he was done with him, he tossed him in the corner.

Eddie's real problem now lied in the fact that he wouldn't see the sunshine outside that prison until Ernesto Salazar was apprehended, and the money he had stolen was recovered. Ernesto was his partner, if you can call him that. He was more of the brains behind the operation, Eddie was the tool to get the job done.

Anyway, according to Eddie it seems Ernesto had made off with all the money in their credit card fraud operation, and Eddie needed me to find him. The outcome of that case didn't pan out well for Eddie. I did what I could to track down his former partner, but Ernesto had left the Caymans the day Eddie was apprehended. Talk about an inside trader, to buy himself some time he probably made the call pointing police right to Eddie. This guy was cold enough to throw his mother to the wolves if he thought it would buy him a five second head start.

By the time I located him, Ernesto had made the move to Brazil. The weather is always nice in Natal, but I don't believe that was his reason for moving there. Brazil had no extradition agreement with the U.S., and that made it even more appealing to Mr. Salazar. There was nothing I could do for Eddie other than to tell him where he could send Ernesto's Christmas card. Yeah, I had located him, that was our agreement, but it didn't do Eddie any good.

Eddie was a likable guy once you got to know him, and I never liked the way that played out at all. He still paid somehow for the investigative work. He even told me he appreciated everything I did for him. I thought *yeah right*, when he said the check is in the mail. I used that on more than one occasion myself. Sure enough, five days later, I received a package. Inside was a check for three grand attached to a personal note, and a Wade Boggs signed baseball. The note said, I know you like baseball. Thought you might want this. Thanks Pepper, signed Eddie. That was the only time he probably signed his real name. The signature on the check was someone else's, but Eddie vouched that it was good.

Anyway, I felt bad about the whole situation, but there was nothing I could do to change it. I'm a private detective, not God. The baseball was a nice touch though. So much, that I had to call to thank him, once the check cleared of course. That was the last time I spoke to Eddie.

I didn't know what the kid knew about him other than he was her uncle. I just knew where he was, he couldn't do anything for her. It figured he'd stick her with me, but at least there was an aunt out there somewhere that could possibly take care of her, and I was bound and determined to find her. "Does your aunt have the same last name as you and your uncle?"

"I guess so."

"Let me guess, you've never seen her."

"Nope."

"Ah, this is just great."

That's when she asked, "do you have a bathroom? I need to go."

Chapter 10

The Clock Was Ticking

Immediately, I stopped what I was doing, and escorted her out of my office, and down the hall to use the facilities. I felt a bit odd waiting outside the door to the women's room, but here I was a grown forty some odd year old man whistling a random tune, looking around as if the hallway I traveled through countless times before was some kind of interesting place to be. I took in the scenery almost like it was a museum filled with exquisite artwork except the paintings were missing, and in there place were suite numbers and company names gracing the wall next to the doors.

In a moment I like to refer to as becoming intimately familiar with your hallway, as uncomfortable as it may be, I checked the time on my watch. She had been in there for more than fifteen minutes. She was definitely female. I rapped on the door yelling, "hey. Is everything okay in there?"

Placing my ear to the door, I heard the water running as she yelled, "yeah, I'm okay."

Shoot me for being a detective, but I had to ask the next question. "What's going on in there?" That's about the time a gentleman I'd never seen before stepped out of one of the offices. He looked over at me probably figuring me for some kind of weirdo. I pointed toward the door with my thumb trying to explain my situation. "You see, there's a girl in there. I mean, I'm just waiting." The look on the guy's face turned even more peculiar as I spoke, so, I stopped while I was ahead.

I did what any guy would do at that point, looked in the other direction and pretended the whole explanation thing never took place. By the time I turned around the guy was gone. A minute later, Kelsey opened the door and informed me the bathroom was gross. I didn't know if the kid had just inspected it thoroughly, or cleaned the entire thing from top to bottom with as much time as she spent in there. "Is that what took you so long," I asked.

"What did you do, time me or something?"

I did, I guess, but I wasn't about to tell her that. "All I know is it took forever."

"No, it didn't."

"Yes, it did."

She looked up at me as we walked back to my office, and she changed the inflection in her voice as she again said, "no, it didn't."

Suddenly, I felt as though I was back on the school playground arguing with another second grader. I wasn't though, I was the adult. So, I acted accordingly. Trying to set a good example, I rephrased my point. "I'm just saying it took a little longer than I expected, that's all."

Kelsey fired back with, "I had to wash my hands. Do you wash your hands when you go?"

"Of course."

"No, you don't."

"Yes, I do."

"No you don't."

"Ah, yes. I do."

"Every time? I don't think so. Next time you go I'm timing you."

"No, you're not."

"Yes, I am."

"You don't even have a watch."

"I'll use yours."

"No you won't."

"Yes I will, watch."

Opening the door to my office to let her inside, I couldn't turn the knob quick enough as I said, "oh God, we have to find your aunt kid."

I walked straight over to my desk, now fully prepared to find this missing Aunt Rhea belonging to Kelsey, assuming she really existed. Eddie had a way of creating people that didn't exist right out of thin air. That was his gift, and that was also my biggest fear.

Chapter 11

More Than I Could Handle

Searching through the rearranged papers on my desk seeing Mrs. Burke's phone number, I realized I needed to call her back to set up a time to meet with her. I still needed a work address for her husband, and most importantly, I needed a retainer something desperate. I don't like to admit it, but I was down to less than a hundred dollars to my name including what was in two checking accounts, my wallet, and both front pockets of the trousers I had been wearing for the past two days.

If there's anything I needed sooner rather than later, that would be a paying case to work. Mrs. Burke's case fit that bill at least. I planned on using it to pay some of my immediate bills. The ones that were past due of course. To complicate things further, it now appeared I had another mouth to feed until I could locate the girl's aunt. Life just never ceases to amaze me. That call to Mrs. Burke would have to wait though.

Just about the time I sat back down in my chair, I heard the door to my office open. I wasn't expecting anyone, but why should that have mattered. I wasn't expecting the seven year old kid either. Kelsey was back at her workstation finishing stacking the pile of papers when I looked over my desk to see a woman standing just inside the door to my office. "Can I help you," I asked.
She responded with, "you're Pepper, I take it."

I stood nodding my head telling her yes, and she informed

me Wally had told her where she could find me. That's when I stepped out from behind my desk, and walked into the other room where the woman was to speak with her face to face, leaving Kelsey to her paper sorting duties. I listened while the woman elaborated on why she was in need of a private investigator.

I'll go ahead and tell you, Wally was my contact down at the police station. He was a good guy that would do just about anything I asked him to, simply for the adrenaline rush, given adequate motivation. I guess you could say he was my information source to everything the police had on record.

He often thought of himself as my partner, even though he wasn't on the payroll. Wally would never help out for the sake of making a buck. In fact, that was one of the things I liked about him. The guy wouldn't take any money even if you offered it, not that I ever did mind you. No, Wally made his living off the taxpayers, and he was honest. He was rare indeed.

A lot of the cases he steered my way cost me time and money, and never paid a dime. Usually, I still took them though. Why? Okay, like I said Wally was a stand-up guy. He liked to help if he could, and I did my part to help Wally out if he knew someone in need of my services. Besides, it was good for business, one pro bono case brought two or three more paying customers through my door. I'll go ahead and tell you this lady wasn't one of them.

She first explained her husband had passed away five months earlier. Then she claimed, "police have deemed the death a suicide which in a way is great because I'm no longer a suspect."

I didn't hear a great deal of sorrow in her voice, but it had been five months since her husband checked out. Perhaps she didn't love him any longer, or she just overcame her grief. Not knowing a damn thing about the man she was married to, made it hard to determine on the surface. Maybe a congratulation was in order, but I just kind of looked at her saying, "alright. So, why do you need me?"

I could feel that small pair of eyes staring at my back from the other room. Without even looking over my shoulder I said, "if you're done with that stack you can work on the one next to it kid." The woman's facial expression changed, but her eyes remained trained on me. I explained, "new secretary, trying to train her, go on."

"Oh well, the problem is the insurance company."

"Always is, isn't it."

"Yes, well it seems they have a clause in the life insurance policy that says they don't have to pay the beneficiary the death benefit in the case of suicide."

"Yes, I'm aware of it."

The woman drew a heavy breath letting it go admitting, "well I wasn't, not until I contacted them several times after I sent them a copy of the death certificate. I really need that money. My husband left me with a huge mortgage, and quite a few bills."

"I'm afraid I can't help you change the course of events Mrs…"

"Oh, I'm sorry, Delores Grayson. I didn't even think to introduce myself. This thing has me so upset."

"I understand. Losing someone close to you like that is tough, I know. You have my condolences."

"Well thank you."

"Have you contacted an attorney? Maybe they can help. I mean, it sounds like a job for them, not a P.I. like me."

"Oh no. I think you misunderstand me. I don't want to try to fight the insurance company with an attorney. I know I'd never win that battle. I only want your help in proving my husband's death was an accident."

This time, I did look over my shoulder. This wasn't the kind of thing I thought a kid should overhear, but I was fairly certain she was listening to every word. I would have been if I were her, but not much that went on inside that office was fit for a kid to be exposed to, and Mrs. Grayson was talking suicide, and now accidental death. At least she wasn't claiming someone killed her husband. The word murder was never mentioned, but this wasn't good. What was worse is she didn't have any money she could pay me to work the case.

She elaborated some about her financial predicament, like that was supposed to convince me to help her. The way she explained it, she was falling behind on her bills. She was desperate. That's the way she put it to me, and she needed that insurance money to square things away, then she could pay me for my efforts.

She did what she could to make her offer sound attractive. "I'll do virtually anything if you can help me." The tone in her voice changed some when she said it. I got her drift, though I never showed it. If she said something like that to Wally she would've had him tripping all over his file folders, me I'm another story.

I had seen my share of women in dire need, and I was no stranger to her indecent proposal. Truthfully, I seldom tired of hearing those pleas. Women are naturally gifted at the art of seduction it seems, but this woman just lost her husband a few months prior to entering my office. She would latch onto any man that could give her what she wanted. I, for one, wasn't about to take advantage of that situation. I have a strict rule regarding client involvement. The rule is, it never happens. You always distance yourself from the client no matter how hot, horny or desperate they may be. Keep it in your pants until the case is closed. That was some of the best advice Willard ever shared with me. Still, to some guys that offer would sound quite appealing.

I didn't wish to take the case in the first place, and of course, I didn't like the sound of that deal. Last man to be paid is always last man out of luck in my world. She wasn't upper-crust, I could tell by her speech, but she dressed well for a woman with little means. I tend to notice things like that at first glance. Delores Grayson wore silk, and nestled snugly between the lapels of her cashmere coat was plenty of cleavage. Being a man I tend to notice things like that as well. Avoid flirting with trouble and look elsewhere Pepper. I told myself that as I watched her take a deep breath. The kid being in the next room was considerably helpful at that point. I had only broken the sacred client rule once, and it came back to bite me. I didn't plan on making that mistake with Mrs. Grayson.

She had to go and pull Wally into it at that point, claiming he said I was the kind of guy that lived to help people. By people she was referring to herself. I can't blame her for playing the defeated widow behind the eight ball card. Fact is, it worked on most people, but I already had more than I could handle with the kid, a missing aunt, and the suspected cheating spouse of Mrs. Burke. Mrs. Grayson would have to wait if I decided to help her out at all because her money problems were not about to help eliminate mine.

Chapter 12

Case Of The Dead Guy

Kelsey was peeping around the edge of the door at me as Mrs. Grayson looked over my shoulder at her. "Oh, I didn't realize you had a little person in your office. I guess I should have called first."

"That's okay, just leave me a number where I can reach you. If I have some time in my schedule in the next few days I'll get a hold of you, and we can discuss your case in detail."

"Okay, here's my card, and I apologize again for the intrusion."

"That's alright, I'll be in touch."

I glanced at her business card as she spoke. "Thank you, thank you so much."

I felt the need to let her know where I stood prior to her leaving my office. "I'm not saying I'll take the case. You understand that, right?"

"Yes, of course." She agreed with what I said, but she looked desperate adding, "I look forward to hearing from you."

Once she left my office, I turned facing Kelsey still holding the business card Mrs. Grayson had given me. Taking another quick look at it I read her job title. From the sound of it she made a good salary, senior business analyst is what it read. The company she worked for I wasn't thoroughly familiar with, but they did something along the lines of product procurement, and international shipping. My guess is she was doing better than me. I was fairly certain she had a nice retirement plan, and plenty of insurance that came with that position within the company life, health, and otherwise.

When I looked up the kid was no longer in sight. That's when I stuck my head inside the other room to see her standing by the perfectly stacked piles of paper. I didn't have a chance to ask her what she had heard, I figured she heard pretty much everything. That's when she said, "all done. Now, can we work on a real case?"

"Not hardly kid."

"Why not? What about the dead guy?"

"The dead guy as you call him was Mr. Grayson, and we're not about to go digging him up."

"Have you ever touched a dead person?"

"Let's talk about something else, shall we."

"You have, haven't you? Mitchell Turner touched a dead bird once. It was nasty."

"Most dead things are, but that's what I call a dead case."

"What do you mean?"

"That case is already solved."

"How did he die?"

"I don't know. It's none of my business."

"I thought you were a detective?"

"I am."

"No, you're not."

"Hey, don't start this again."

"Start what?"

"This."

"You don't make any sense sometimes."

"Yeah, well the feeling is mutual kid."

"What's mutual?"

"Do you ever run out of questions?"

"How come you can ask questions?"

"There you go again, cause I'm a detective. It's my job to ask questions. That's how you find out stuff."

"Well, I'm a kid and it's my job to ask questions too.

You're no detective though."

"Why do you say that?"

"Because you don't even know how he died, and you're afraid to touch dead people."

"I leave that job to the coroner."

"Who's that?"

"He's the guy that gets paid to touch dead people."

"I don't want his job."

"Me either kid. Now find something to do in the other room for a minute while I make a call, okay."

She looked depressed as she turned moping out of my office. I didn't think kids could get depressed. They haven't been around long enough to let life get to them to wear them down, but what the kid had been through, or seen, I didn't know for sure. My guess was someone close to her had died because death certainly wasn't a foreign concept to her. I watched her plop down on my sofa, and pick up a magazine to thumb through it as I dialed Mrs. Burke back to go ahead, and get her case underway.

Chapter 13

Short On Patience And Money

It was looking as though I was going to need the money. Listening to the phone ring, I waited impatiently thinking to myself, I had to be the brokest guy in Boston with more work than I could handle. The problem was this was the only case that had the possibility of paying something up front, so you know it got my full attention.

Mrs. Burke answered the phone, and I told her I could meet her at her earliest convenience. She sounded highly motivated at that point, so I also mentioned I needed a work address for her husband, and his general schedule if she wanted me to proceed with the investigation. She didn't hesitate providing me with either. That's when I threw in that I could start working the case as soon as I was paid five hundred up front. I felt like I had short changed myself when she asked, "is that all?"

You know what they say, some work is better than no work, but paid work is best, hands down. I clarified my position with Mrs. Burke telling her the entire bill for her case shouldn't exceed two thousand dollars. My guess was it would be in the neighborhood of fifteen hundred. I explained, "I just require the five hundred up front to begin surveillance." That was alright with her. Why wouldn't it be? It was her husband's money she was spending to have him tailed.

Mrs. Burke said, "I'll be at your office at two o' clock this afternoon, if that's a good time."

I looked over at the kid sitting on the sofa, and I had no idea how I was going to juggle her, and Mrs. Burke as I said, "oh, two o' clock will be fine. I'll see you then." That's when she asked for directions to my office. I tried my best to tell her where I was, and how to get there before ending the call, but street names and general directions like north and east didn't really register with her. She relied more on landmarks to get to where she was going. Thank God for jewelry stores, hair salons, restaurants, boutiques, and specialty shops. It took several attempts on my part, but with the help of Natick Mall, and Copley Place, I managed to point her in the right direction.

As I hung up the phone, I looked at the notepad which I had jotted down her husband's work address on. Kelsey took that opportunity to tell me she was hungry. It was just after twelve, and my stomach was starting to rumble too. "Come on kid, I know a place where we can grab something to eat pretty cheap."
"Do they have milkshakes?"
"No, I don't think so."
"What do they have?"
"You like hotdogs?"
"Sure."
"They have plenty of those. Let's go."

On my way out of the office, I grabbed my coat and hat. The kid looked at me asking, "why are you taking that? It's not that cold outside."
"I'm a detective, it's part of my uniform."
"You don't have a uniform."
"Okay. Well, I never leave my office without my coat and hat. How about that?"
The kid shrugged her shoulder as she followed me down the steps. Needless to say, she didn't navigate the stairs

quite the same way I did. She preferred to hop down each one counting them out loud as she went. Everything was a game to her. I looked at her, and asked, "do you see me hopping?"

She looked at me with an innocent expression saying, "no, but you should try it. It's fun, see." She took another small leap, and she looked up at me.

I firmly said, "stop doing that and hold the handrail." I sounded like my former school bus driver when I was in grammar school. That's when she informed me I was no fun at all. "I'm not a clown kid. I'm a what?"

"A fuddy-duddy."

I just looked at her the way Willard used to look at me when I cracked wise about something. It appeared I had that look down cold. I delivered it to witnesses on many an occasion when I knew they were withholding information worth having. So, I had plenty of practice, enough to force the kid to say, "I know you're a detective."

"That's right, and detectives don't hop, jump or skip. Got it?"

"Got it."

"Good. I'm glad we got that straightened out."

Just as I turned thinking we had resolved that little matter, she asked me another question as I started back down the steps. "Can I wear your hat?"

"No."

"Why not?"

"Cause someone might mistake you for a detective which you're not."

The kid held the handrail as she took another leap down to the next step. Holding my hat in my hand, I gave her my I mean business look. That's when she made me an offer I couldn't refuse as she said, "if you let me wear your hat I promise I'll stop hopping."

I took the old gray wool felt fedora I held in my hand, and I placed it on top of the kid's head as I said, "deal. Watch your step and give me your hand."

"How do I look?"

"You look like a short private investigator, what else."

She found that funny, at least she laughed. She couldn't see the expression I had on my face at that moment, but I found her rather amusing. The hat covered her eyes when she looked straight ahead. Her feet and the steps beneath them had to be just about the only thing she could see while wearing the hat. All I knew was it momentarily kept her from hopping and asking questions, counting steps that was another story.

Chapter 14

Making The Rounds

Teddy was the first to notice the kid as I brought her down the stairs. That wasn't surprising though, not much slipped passed Teddy. He was sitting in his chair reading over the paper as he said, "about time you showed up. I was beginning to wonder about you."

Teddy glanced at his watch when I said, "I've been a little busy."

"I see that. Who do we have here?"

"Better take the hat off kid. I told you no one would recognize you wearing it." Kelsey lifted the hat from her head looking up at Teddy, and I introduced them to one another. "She was sent to me special delivery. Can you believe that?"

"Well, how about that. So, now you have a new partner, I take it."

"Just until we locate her aunt."

"That should be as easy as pulling money out of this hat, I imagine."

Teddy took that opportunity to wow the kid with his slight of hand as he reached toward my hat, and magically pulled a fifty cent piece from it. The kid's eyes widened, and her mouth opened slightly as she stared at it a second. She started to ask how he did it just before Teddy handed her the shiny silver coin saying, "you don't want to leave this in there. It's good luck. You hold on to it until you and Pepper find your aunt."

Teddy never ceased to amaze me. He was good with the

kid, for an old shine man, you know. "It's that time," I said looking right at him.

"Yeah, so it is. It's your turn to buy isn't it?"

I subtly laughed at that one. One way or another I always ended up buying. Teddy was an almanac of sports facts, and quick with a two headed coin toss, but like every day around lunchtime, I made him an offer he couldn't refuse. He lived off of Joe's hotdogs and bratwurst just like me. Over the years, we had become Joe's best customers, and consumed God knows how many pounds of beef franks, and pork sausages. "We're going to grab some lunch. Want us to bring you back something?"

"I'll take two all the way with extra slaw."

"I figured you'd say that."

As we left, Kelsey looked back over her shoulder at Teddy. She was trying to figure him out, I suppose. Teddy was comfortably seated back in his chair reading his paper by the time we reached the front doors of the building. He waved to the kid as I opened the door for her, and it appeared he had made a new friend with a simple greeting combined with his nifty coin trick.

Halfway to Joe's hotdog stand all I heard was one question after another about Teddy. They ranged from whether or not Teddy was some kind of magician to the names of his grandkids. She wanted to know everything about him it seemed. What her fascination was with Teddy, I couldn't begin to understand. I guess cheap magic tricks make quite an impression on young kids.

Whatever information I did give her about Teddy only led to another question. Eventually, I got wise to the fact that regardless of what I shared with her there would always be another question to follow. That's when I went with the, "I don't know," response promptly followed by the, "I don't know that either," retort. Give the kid three or four of those back to back, and she'd point blank ask you, "well, what do you know?" All I learned from the childish interrogation was there was still a great deal I really didn't know about Teddy, which was odd in a way. We had been friends going on sixteen years at that point. I could tell you what he was thinking half the time just by the look he had in his eye, and he could often complete my sentences. We knew each other quite well in my opinion, or so I thought. It just never occurred to me to ask how old his grandchildren were, or what their names were even, and I called myself a detective.

I still knew the names of Mrs. Abrams children cause she called them by name as she scolded them for running in the house as I interviewed her briefly two years prior. I hadn't spoken to her since that first meeting, but I even managed to retain her kids' ages along with their favorite activities. It was information I didn't ask for, but she divulged in the course of conversation. Strange part was I probably spent less than seven minutes talking to her amid all the chaos, and the fact was I knew more about her family than I did about Teddy's. Oh, and that was virtually nothing compared to what I learned about people sharing public transportation. Some of them were open books when it came to their personal business. Obviously, there was still much to learn about the old shine guy that steered me into becoming a P.I.

The facts were if a case paid money I dug for information. Outside of that, I really didn't care to know anything personal about people. I mean if they shared something with me in a passing conversation my memory would lock it away automatically, but other than that I didn't pry into people's lives. That just wasn't my thing. It was too much like work, I guess. You can probably understand that.

Besides, Teddy and I talked about important stuff like cases I was working, or what the word was on the street about certain individuals connected to them, and we talked sports of course, like I said the important stuff.

What was most important at that point was the Boston Red Sox were only four games away from making it to the World Series. That was phenomenal in my book. I could've never predicted that at the start of the season, but there were many things about the future I hadn't planned on, Kelsey being one of them. Here I was stuck with a kid, and what was shaping out to be a heavy case load while my favorite team was on the brink of making baseball history. I could hear the sports analysts making their comments on the radio as we approached Joe's hotdog stand. The Sox were in for a heavy match up it seemed.

Changing the subject I told Kelsey, "Teddy's not only the Beantown checker champ two years running, he's also a sports aficionado." She, of course, had no idea what that was. I told her Teddy had the uncanny ability to retain any sports statistics he came across, and I began to explain the significance of this upcoming game, but I could tell she wasn't impressed.

Joe saw us coming half a block away. He pulled out a fresh bun and raised his hand holding a set of tongs ready to fill my order. He looked pleasantly surprised to see me walking beside my new travel companion. Against my better judgment, I took that opportunity to introduce the kid to America's greatest pastime expounding on the intense rivalry between the Red Sox and the Yankees. To be honest, I expected her to start yawning at that moment, but she actually became quite ecstatic. Shocking, I know. No, she wasn't a fan of baseball, but she evidently had a thing for animals, one in particular. What had Kelsey's interest had four legs, plenty of hair, a scruffy face and a crooked tale. That was Joe's dog, of course. Joe like to call him Cheeseburger, and I called him anything that came to mind whenever he looked up at me from the pavement.

Joe was a unique individual. On the surface, to most of his customers, he probably seemed like an average Joe, no pun intended, but the fact was Joe had a keen sense of insight when it came to people. To define him in one breath I'd have to say he sold a lot of hotdogs, and watched way too much television, but in a pinch occasionally he was helpful in solving cases. That stays between you me though, no need to let Joe in on that little tidbit.

Truth is he sold bratwurst, and I ate them like they were going out of style all while picking his brain just to see what he thought about something. Joe never was the wiser. Cheeseburger, on the other hand knew plenty, mostly how to make you feel sorry for him, but he had a dozen tricks in his repertoire, and he'd use every last one of them if it meant sampling some of your hotdog.

Joe hollered, "you're late."
"I know. I see you and the dog waited for me though."
"You know Cheeseburger, he's always ready to sell another hotdog. I see you brought someone along with you."
"Yeah. Tell him your name kid."

Kelsey took her eyes off Cheeseburger long enough to spit out her name. It was obvious what her focus was on as Joe introduced himself, and welcomed her to his hotdog stand for the first time. Kelsey asked, "is that your dog?"
Joe smirked as he said, "yeah, but he likes to think of

himself as my partner since everyone comes here to see him, not me. His name is Cheeseburger."

"For real?"

"Well, what did you expect me to call him, hotdog? That could get a little confusing around here, now couldn't it? I wouldn't know if someone wanted to buy one of these or my partner over there. He's not for sale by the way."

The kid smiled at Joe as she asked, "can I pet him?" That's when Joe looked up at me.

"After you eat kid."

"What's it going to be today," Joe asked. "I hope you brought your appetite." Joe knew I always came ready to eat, his loaded bratwursts were my weakness.

I said, "I'll take one all the way, and the kid here likes hotdogs."

Joe pulled a steaming wiener out of his cart, and he placed it on the bun saying, "well, she's in luck. I just happen to have plenty of those."

"That's what I told her." Joe asked what she wanted on it, but Kelsey didn't answer. She was still distracted staring at Cheeseburger as he sat at attention waiting for something good to eat.

I asked, "you like ketchup and mustard kid?"

"Yeah."

Joe dressed it up to perfection and handed it to her saying, "that's called a regular, throw some pickle relish on there and then you got a classic."

Kelsey grinned at him before saying, "thanks," and I watched her take a huge bite as Joe reached for another bun. The dog appeared as though he was waiting to help her finish it, but that was just the start of a faithful friendship.

Chapter 15

Long On Hope

The kid walked over to say hey to Cheeseburger, and I told her, "whatever you do, don't feed the dog." Joe just laughed under his breath as he fixed my bratwurst just how I liked it. We both listened to the pre-game show on the radio.

Joe spoke with some enthusiasm when he said, "hard to believe we're this close, huh."

Everyone in Boston was a Sox fan no matter who you were. For guys like me and Joe, this game meant something. It was important, it was our chance at greatness even though neither of us made the roster. We were certainly there in spirit though. We loved the sound of the crack of the bat, there were no two ways about it. They should have given us jerseys just for our unwavering support. It was probably our prayers, and positive thoughts that propelled the team to this point I thought as I said, "yeah, I just hope they don't screw it up."

Joe just nodded his head adding, "if anyone can, it would be them."

Hey, Joe was a pretty straight forth kind of guy. If something entered his mind it left his lips, it's just that simple. So, maybe we weren't always a hundred percent positive, but we were Red Sox fans through and through. No one could deny us that title.

That was something a seven year old girl couldn't begin to understand. She was young with a lot of life left ahead of her. She had plenty of time left to see her favorite team take home the trophy. In her case, that team would probably one day consist of two very graceful figure skaters wearing matching outfits covered in sequins, but the point is she had time.

For Joe and me it was different, we were… Well, we weren't young let's put it that way, and don't even get me started on where Teddy fell in that equation. As for the Boston Red Sox winning the World Series, none of us had seen it happen in our lifetime, and Teddy was old, there's just no other way to say it.

Trying to get nine guys on a baseball field to work together as a finely tuned machine was no easy feat, not for my team anyway. Francona had his work cut out for him, but Joe and I, we had hope.

Cheeseburger held out hope as well, hoping something tasty would leave Kelsey's fingers, and hit the sidewalk where it was all his. All I can say is she didn't leave him hoping for long before she fulfilled his very wish. One little trick, and he had the kid wrapped around his dewclaw, but Cheeseburger was a ham. He liked to show-off. First, he led with a paw in the air, then he placed it over the bridge of his nose. That's when I saw the first piece hit the concrete. From there God only knows what the dog did to keep the hotdog coming. I'm telling you that canine was a pro. The stand-up turn around got me every time. I finally had to stop looking at him altogether. It was costing me too much money. Anyway the dog lived well, and Joe didn't fare too bad either.

Chapter 16

Joe's Advice

Making our predictions, Joe and I coached the game from his hotdog stand while the kid played a game of her own which was feeding Cheeseburger when she thought no one was looking. She actually spent more time feeding her hotdog to Cheeseburger than she did eating it. Joe watched her out of the corner of his eye right along with me as she made Cheeseburger's day pinching off pieces of her hotdog feeding it to him whenever our heads would turn in the other direction. Alright, it was cheap fun. Joe pointed out, "the kid likes dogs. Maybe you should get her one."

"I'm not planning on keeping her that long."

"Well Cheeseburger sure will miss her when you stop bringing her around."

"Yeah, I guess you'll have to feed him yourself."

"Does that dog look like he's ever missed a meal."

"No. I'd say not."

"Yeah, but I can tell that hotdog must taste even better coming from her."

"Well that's how it is with everything you're not supposed to have isn't it?"

"That's right. You working another case?"

"Yeah. I've got to meet a client in about an hour."

"What's the story with the kid?"

"Got to find her aunt."

"Aren't you the busy man."

"Busy and broke as ever."

"Nah, not you Pepper. All those cases, you have to be bringing in the cabbage." He scooped up a spoon full of kraut as he asked, "you want some more?"

I just nodded my head saying, "yeah. You know, not all cases pay money, unfortunately."

"Really?"

"Well, some I take on as a favor even when someone can't quite afford to pay me for my time."

"Yeah, like what kind of cases?"

"Well I had a woman come into my office this morning needing someone to investigate her husband's death, and she couldn't pay for my help."

"Did you take the case?"

"I'm still undecided. I need to talk to her, one on one, you know when the kid isn't around just to see what I'm up against."

"I'd be careful if I were you. Do you ever watch that show on TV called Snapped?"

"No. I'm afraid I haven't."

"Well you should. Some of those women on there… Well…" Joe stopped short of finishing his sentence. So, I pressed him.

"Well, what?"

"Well, they snap you know."

"This case isn't like that. The police already cleared her. She just needs me to prove cause of death was an accident."

"Why is that?"

"Insurance proceeds. She needs my help in order to get the money."

"Hey, that's just like this episode I saw. You better watch yourself." Joe glanced over his shoulder at the kid as Cheeseburger finished off the last bite of Kelsey's hotdog, and he looked back at me saying, "I mean some of these women are dangerous, and they are always involved somehow in offing the husbands, usually for the insurance money."

Joe was overly paranoid perhaps. Like I said, he watched

way too much television. He had no intention of getting married just for that reason alone, but the last part of what he said stuck with me. Leave it to him to offer his two cents about a possible pro bono case he knew virtually no details about, and tie insurance money as a motive to Mrs. Grayson doing in her husband. Now, all of a sudden that case bothered me thanks to him. I preferred not to think about it, but it was difficult to dismiss what Joe just said.

Chapter 17

Second Thoughts

I never like prejudging cases before I looked at evidence, and this one I was truly hoping to avoid altogether. What did Joe know? The police obviously deemed the death a suicide. If Mrs. Grayson was involved in any way with her husband's demise, it would certainly be difficult to prove, if not impossible, or she would not have sought out the services of a private investigator.

With that in mind, what police had ruled a suicide, she hoped I could prove was an accident. If I were successful in my efforts she would not only receive her husband's death benefit she would most likely receive double indemnity. That would be a jackpot amount, I was certain of that. That meant she would have plenty of money to pay me, but thanks to Joe's comment something about this case didn't sit right with me without even seeing the first piece of evidence.

Preconceived notions based purely on hunches without facts to substantiate them have no place in my line of work. Sometimes, it was hard to override them though. Possible motive and insurance proceeds aside, I wanted to believe the woman that walked through my door was innocent of any wrongdoing in the death of her husband, but what my gut said was I needed another bratwurst to fill the emptiness I felt deep down inside when I thought of Mrs. Grayson's demeanor, and the lack of feeling she had for her dearly departed husband.

I reflected back on how her voice sounded when we spoke in my office. I replayed it in my head as I stood there listening to the radio announcer with Joe. It was clear to me Mrs. Grayson had pure concern in her voice when she spoke to me about her dilemma. It was also quite clear that concern was for herself, and her financial situation without the use of her husband's insurance money.

Doing the prudent thing at that point, I chose to block that thought out of my mind altogether. Truthfully, I didn't want to know that answer. I didn't know her husband or her for that matter. I also didn't know how well she knew Wally. He sent anyone in the world to me that had a problem. Those people consisted of neighbors, relatives, people he met on the street, and those he came across in the normal course of business. Where Mrs. Grayson fell in that mix I couldn't be sure until I had a chance to talk to him. My hands were full at that moment though. I had a missing aunt to locate, a kid to look after until I accomplished that mission, and a cheating spouse case to work not to mention the loaded bratwurst which filled both hands.

I hope you don't think ill of me, but as a detective it's hard to make a living working cases that cost you money. Working cases where there's no winner in the end never was my bag to begin with, I worked enough of them to know that. Point blank, my batting record was good for this business, and I planned to keep it that way.

Yeah, I know what you're saying. If this did play out the way Joe painted it, what about Mr. Grayson. Hey, there's no bringing him back we all know that, but you're right. If someone did do him in, they needed to be brought to justice, even if that someone happened to be his wife. Mr. Grayson, obviously, had some kind of image when he was living. I don't know what it was exactly, I never had the chance to get to know him. At this point I couldn't tell you anything about him other than his wife's name, but being labeled as someone that committed suicide was no honor. All I knew was I didn't owe him anything.

Maybe Mr. Grayson's death really was an accident, and his wife wasn't trying to put one over on the insurance company. Considering that if I dismissed the thought of working his case simply because it wouldn't pay, that alone, would stick with me for the rest of my life. I had a tendency to carry crap like that around with me. It was just who I was, and I couldn't help that.

Willard told me one time, "that's what will make you great Pepper." He meant it would make me great at uncovering what others refuse to look for, thereby making me a great detective. The part he left out was it will eat you alive if you ever turn your back on that part of you which lies deep within. I had to find that out the hard way several times. This wasn't going to be one of them. I told myself, don't confront the case unless it confronts you. That was the best way to handle it I assure you.

Chapter 18

What People Need Most

I looked over at the kid shaking hands with her four legged pal. Knowing the answer I went ahead and asked her, "are you still hungry?"

"I could eat one more."

"Alright, this time don't feed it to your fury friend there, how about it."

"Oh him, he's full."

"Yeah, I'm sure of that."

"He does neat tricks. I taught him how to shake. See?"

"I see."

Joe suppressed a laugh as he said, "yep, she's quite the dog trainer. Guess you'll have to come see him each day and work with him on a regular basis."

Leave it to Joe to take that opportunity to cultivate another regular customer. I ate there practically every day I was close to the office around lunchtime. Joe said, "I think he wants you to scratch his head." Kelsey proceeded to massage Cheeseburger's scalp with her tiny fingers as the dog's tongue hung in the air and his ears went off high alert. He was obviously enjoying the attention as Joe said in his best dog voice, "oh yeah, that's the spot. Right there, I can never reach that one."

The kid laughed as Joe handed her another hotdog. This one he had thrown some pickle relish on, and he told her, "you can't give him any of this one cause pickles tend to make him gassy."

I had to add, "and that's not good for business."

Kelsey found that amusing as Joe nodded his head in an exaggerated manner. That's when he looked at Kelsey and said, "that would be one dollar." Kelsey looked up at him, and she pulled the fifty cent piece out of her pocket which Teddy had given her to hold as she said, "all I have is this, but I can't give it to you because it belongs to Teddy. It's lucky you know. So, I have to keep it."

Joe looked at Cheeseburger, and then he turned back toward Kelsey saying, "that's okay. Cheeseburger says you are our hundredth customer of the day. He keeps count for me. You know what that means?" The kid shook her head no. Joe informed her the hundredth customer of the day never has to pay for their hotdog, it's free.

Kelsey held the classic hotdog in one hand and her lucky coin in the other as her eyes lit up a little. She believed that coin was lucky alright, and she voiced it out loud, "I knew it was lucky." She looked at it before stuffing it back in her pocket.

This time the thanks went to Cheeseburger, and he graciously accepted the praise. Joe's compliment came in form of a mouth full of hotdog as Kelsey tried to say, "this is good," as she continued chewing.

I figured now was as good a time as any to try my luck as I said, "well, you know I came with her. In fact, I actually brought her here. So, I guess my bratwurst that I'm about to order, and the two I'm taking back for Teddy are covered under that hundredth customer promotion thing you, and Cheeseburger have going, right."

"No, actually that would make you customer one hundred and one."

"And one hundred and one pays full price, right."

"You got it."

"Story of my life, I just can't catch a break."

"Well maybe you should get a lucky coin like the kid."

"I'd settle for one more all the way, and two for Teddy with extra slaw, but short the onions a little."

"What are you his mother?"

"I just like messing with him, you know that."

"Well, I can help you out there, I guess."

Joe fixed Teddy's order according to my instructions. I stood there trying to listen to the game on the radio, but my mind was far removed from it. The Grayson case was also blocked out of my conscious thoughts for the moment. What I did think of was this seven year old animal lover, and her lucky coin. What I thought was merely a well-executed coin trick was something more, in fact.

Apparently, Teddy understood something I didn't about kids, and maybe people in general regardless of their age. What Teddy had a grasp of that I didn't, was everyone needs to have something tangible worth something even if only to them. The kid had a shiny silver piece with John F. Kennedy's head on it. I wouldn't care to wager how lucky that coin was, but to her it was valuable. Teddy had instilled that belief in her when he handed her that coin, and with that he had instilled hope. Hope for what some might ask. I'd say for finding someone or something she could truly count on, someone who could give her a brighter future. Isn't that what most of us are searching for in this life. One thing's certain, Kelsey needed some major improvement in hers, and here she was stuck tagging along with an old gumshoe like me.

The only hope I had was that her aunt would be that person, and that the Sox would put a new pitcher on the mound for the start of the next game to shutout the Orioles, clinching their spot in the World Series. That's when Joe handed me the bag as he called me by name, "Pepper."

I looked over at him asking how much I owed him and he said, "eight ought to get it."

Looking back at Kelsey explaining to Cheeseburger why she couldn't share her hotdog with him, I directed my remark toward Joe saying, "a dog, huh."

Joe's eyebrows raised slightly as his lips protruded a bit. Looking at her he nodded his head. "Most kids love them," he claimed.

I looked down at my watch and back up at the kid. I figured, I could spare a few more minutes letting her converse with Marmaduke before we had to head back, but when the time came to deliver Teddy his lunch, and meet Mrs. Burke, I could tell the kid didn't want to go. I told Joe, I'd see him tomorrow, and he said what he always did whenever we parted company. That was that they'd be looking for me.

The kid followed my lead making sure she said bye to Cheeseburger, and we started back toward my office with Teddy's lunch in hand. On the way there the conversation centered around animals mostly. What I took away from our lengthy talk was Kelsey couldn't wait to go back to Joe's hotdog stand, plain and simple.

Chapter 19

Time Spent With Teddy

We walked up the steps in front of my building, and I handed the bag I was carrying to Kelsey. Teddy was finishing up with a customer as we walked through the doors. It was almost two o' clock, and I was fairly certain he was starving by the look on his face, and the way he shooed that guy out of the chair after seeing us. I figured I'd let the kid hand him his lunch, that way there would be no complaints from Teddy.

Seeing as Mrs. Burke would be there any minute it was also convenient that the kid had a story to share with him about the lucky coin he let her hold. It was perfect, she could tell him all about Joe's dog, and I could step upstairs to meet Mrs. Burke.
"I was beginning to think you two got lost."
"Tell him what happened kid."

Kelsey handed Teddy his lunch, and she started talking his ear off about her free hotdog, the lucky coin and Cheeseburger's performance, but Teddy didn't care, he was hungry.

I watched him a second as he prepared to bite into his bratwurst. He actually appeared to be listening to everything the kid was saying, but it was hard to tell with Teddy, part of his job was to pretend to listen to people. He did it all day long. So, maybe he was what you would call a professional listener. Come on, bartenders and therapists aren't the only ones in this town that have to listen to people's troubles.

Teddy was into tips, and pretending someone had something of interest to share made him plenty. When something really was of interest he usually found a way to make money off of me with that information.

I glanced at my watch as Teddy offered Kelsey a seat in one of his chairs. That's when I pointed upstairs using my thumb saying, "if you don't mind, I have to meet someone. I'll be right back." Teddy looked at me as the kid continued with her story. I could read the look on his face, and I knew what he was about say. Kelsey was right at the good part about how she pulled out her coin and showed it to Joe. I told Teddy to make sure he listened cause he didn't want to miss it as he grumbled about Joe not putting any onions on his bratwurst.

Teddy bellowed, "it never fails. I ask for extra slaw, and he shorts me something. Was he out of onions?"
"No. I had plenty, and they were good, man they were good. I can't believe he didn't give you any."
Teddy nodded his head a bit in utter disgust saying, "that's what brings out the flavor, you know."

If there was one thing I enjoyed it was messing with Teddy. That's when I said, "oops, you missed the best part." I looked over at Kelsey and said, "you better start over kid."
"Kelsey turned looking directly at Teddy with a bit of an exasperated expression on her face as she said, "I thought you were listening."
Teddy answered her back with his mouth half-full of food saying, "I was," but the kid wasn't about to let him off that easy.
Resting her chin on her hand she asked him, "what did I

78

say?"

For once Teddy was at a loss for words. It was priceless. Luckily, I was there to capture the moment with my camera phone. Oh, yeah, Teddy was great with kids, alright. He had much to learn about this one though. Teddy shoved another bite of bratwurst in his mouth as he muttered, "I didn't know there was going to be a test question."

Kelsey looked at me as though she expected me to translate, and I said, "he said, he just heard part of it. Cut him some slack. He's old, and his ears aren't that good, that's the problem, but he wants you to start from the very beginning."

I exchanged a grin with Teddy as he forced himself to swallow. Then he sounded off, "I'll tell you what the problem is," but at that point the kid started telling her story for the second time. She loved telling it, and Teddy had nothing else to do while he ate his lunch. So, I took that opportunity to meet Mrs. Burke.

Chapter 20

In Walked Money

Just about the time I unlocked the door to my office, and took off my coat tossing it over the armrest of the sofa, I could hear what sounded like a pair of Giuseppe Zanotti's coming down the hall heading toward my door. I know what you're probably saying to yourself, nobody's ears are that good. Well, I know the sound of money when I hear it coming that's for sure, and as far as ears go, mine are exceptional. Let's just leave it at that for now.

Those footsteps I heard stopped just as I turned toward the door, and there stood Mrs. Burke dressed in what looked like a high end designer pantsuit with a contrasting camisole. It had a herringbone pattern if I remember correctly, and I believe the color itself was peach orchard. Hey, don't go getting the wrong idea about me just because I occasionally pick up a women's fashion magazine every now and then. It's important to stay abreast of the latest trends you know. It's helpful in this business. How else can you expect to accurately describe a suspect to someone on the street, or better yet gain a true perspective from them as to what someone truly looked like?

Okay, maybe that much detail wasn't always required to pin down who exactly you were looking for, but those magazines were in every office waiting area throughout Boston. My work took me to those places not to mention numerous hair salons. You try passing the time waiting to speak to a hairstylist or the shampoo girl without picking one up to peruse through it. It's damn difficult, I say impossible. Frankly, the women on the covers are always hot. Now that you know where I gained my education in the world of fashion, back to the client, Mrs. Burke. As I greeted her with a pleasant, "hello," my eyes met hers.

"You are Pepper, I presume."

"Yes." I glanced down at my watch as I added, "it looks like you're right on time Mrs. Burke. Come on in."

Normally, I allowed the client to introduce themselves whenever we first met to avoid divulging their name to the wrong person, unless I recognized their voice, or they were there at an appointed time holding a check in their hand as it happened to be the case with Mrs. Burke.

She was ready to get the show on the road. So was I, I had bills to pay. Mr. Burke, well he was on his own at that point. At least for his sake he should have prayed he was alone, but I had strong doubts that was the case.

Mrs. Burke was a fairly attractive woman especially for her age, but money had the ability to keep women beautiful well into their later years. She didn't appear to be hurting for any. She was also out for blood. That was quite clear, but she did it with flare. I had to hand her credit there. She had certainly overcome distraught as she said, "I always try to be punctual. Fortunately for me, I didn't even have to tap." She was referring to knocking on my door, but tap was the word she chose to express that action. Translation, this woman had money.

I gave a halfhearted chuckle at her remark, trying to keep the mood in the room as light as possible under the circumstances. I looked down at the check which she had handed me. Holding it in my hand, I noticed my first mistake as my eyes stared down in the direction of the floor.

I could see she wasn't wearing Giuseppe Zanotti's, those were Salvatore Ferragamo's she had on her feet. At over five hundred dollars a pair, I knew right away I had way under-priced this one.

If I were a woman, which I'm obviously not, and those shoes were my size, I'd have probably made out better trading out my services for the shoes instead of the retainer she was bringing to me. They were nice, that's all I'm saying. What, a guy can't appreciate tasteful footwear, and women's fashion? I'm a private detective not a caveman for God's sake.

My meeting with Mrs. Burke went pretty well. Sometimes meeting with a jilted spouse could be dicey, it could cost me a box of tissues or a new windowpane to go in my office door depending on their emotional state. This time it was all business. I think she already envisioned Mr. Burke in the courtroom when the judge signed the papers giving her the house and everything else under the sun he had worked his entire life to acquire.

The sharp stick in the eye at that point would be the future earnings Mr. Burke would never see thanks to the substantial alimony check he'd have to continue to write for the rest of his life. Yep, leave it to Mrs. Burke to come up with a much better retirement plan than Charles Schwab could have ever given her.

Chapter 21

Life Through Kelsey's Eyes

With Mrs. Burke's check in hand it was time to hit the bank, get some cash, pay a bill, check on the kid, and see how Teddy was holding up, not necessarily all in that order. By the time I made it back downstairs Teddy had finished his lunch, and the kid had told him her story probably more than once. They got along good, those two. It was scary actually, but Teddy had another customer waiting to get a shine, and I was right on time to take the kid off his hands so he could get back to what he did best, which was polishing shoes and taking people's money.

I expected some kind of grief from Teddy about how long it took for me to handle things with Mrs. Burke, but to my surprise he didn't grumble a bit about watching Kelsey for me. Teddy got up from his chair so his customer could take a seat, and he reached for his rag as I said, "alright kid, we have some place to be. So, let's go. Thanks for watching her for me Teddy."

"No problem," was all he said to me, but he made sure to tell Kelsey he'd see her later. That's when the kid informed me she liked Teddy.

I played dumb, rather convincingly I might add, as I said, "really, I couldn't tell."

"Yeah, his name reminds me of a teddy bear. How about you?"

I have to admit Teddy never brought to my mind an image of a teddy bear, but I wasn't seven either. After her making the comparison I'd probably never see him the same again.

Kids, I guess, see things different than guys like me nearing their prime. Yeah, I said prime. Humor me some if you will. I had been on the verge of reaching my prime my entire life, and I refused to surpass it regardless of my age. I wasn't about to start then and fess up to the best years of my life being behind me. I wasn't suffering from low 'T' just yet. Maybe on the verge, but in my mind I'd be nearing my prime if I made it to ninety-nine. That's what kept me young on the inside. Forget about the exterior, there was little hope for that hanging in there for the long haul.

P.I.s usually didn't fare well after fifty, physically anyway. Too many hours of sleep lost, cheap booze, fast food and poor exercise tended to take its toll at that time. Fortunately for me, I had a few good years left in me at that point. Here's to good health.

To answer the kid, I glanced back over my shoulder at Teddy as I said, "yeah, I guess he is just a silly old bear." Winnie the Pooh popped in my mind as I watched him go to town shining those shoes. I had the overwhelming urge to call him pooh-bear next time I saw him, but I figured I'd save it for the right moment.

"Where are we going," the kid asked. No, she didn't lose her inquisitive side while hanging out with Teddy - that was quite clear.

"I need to run an errand or two, thought you might want to come along with me."

"Can we get a milkshake?"

"We'll see," I said as I looked down at her while she walked with me to my car. The expression on her face changed slightly. It was sort of funny to me, but the kid proved to me she was no dummy with her remark as she said, "I know what that means. No."

Not wishing to lie to the kid, and to teach her one should

mean exactly what they say, I took it upon myself to set a fine example for her when I replied, "No, would mean no. We'll see means, we will see."

"What's that supposed to mean, exactly?"

I thought I made my point quite clear, but Kelsey didn't hold any affinity for possibly, maybe or we'd just have to leave things to fate to see what happens when it came to whether or not she was going to get a milkshake.

I can't blame her there cause milkshakes are good, hell everyone knows that. The kid appreciated definite answers when it came to the important things in her world. I could respect that. I kind of liked to know a few things myself without question, like whether or not the Red Sox were going to win the pennant, and if this Aunt Rhea of hers really existed. All I said to her at that point was, "you still have your lucky coin, don't you."

As we approached my car a slight grin somehow made its way to her little face as she said with absolute certainty, "yep, we're getting milkshakes."

I went to open the door for her as I said, "we'll see," just to add a degree of suspense, and not give the kid the impression I was an absolute pushover which we all know I'm not. Right?

That's when she took one look at my car and asked, "that's it?"

"That's it. You're looking at one of America's finest cars to ever hit the road. There's 271 horses under that hood. That's a rare thing to come by in a classic V8. Trust me whatever you're out to catch, you can do it in this baby."

She looked it over as I described it. All she said at first was, "it could use a wash. I can clean it for you, I think." She paused another second or two then she went with, "I can try."

"That's not necessary. This is a surveillance vehicle, it's supposed to not draw attention."

Her eyes went to one side as her mouth pulled toward the other, and she asked, "how come we're taking it now, are we going on a case?"

"No. We're headed to the bank, the case comes later."

"Then how come we're going in this car?"

She tried to say surveillance, but the word came out somewhat discombobulated and garbled. I didn't bother to correct her. I just replied, "cause this is the only one we've got right now. You want to get in?"

She paused a second as if she was mulling that one over as she looked inside. I mentioned it was a classic, and she looked up at me. You know the old saying a picture is worth a thousand words, well her face spoke volumes, she got in though.

Like I said the kid wasn't dumb, she knew she didn't really have a choice. If she wanted a milkshake this was the only way to get to it. Honestly after getting to know her, I believe the kid would have hopped a northbound train, stowed away on a slow boat to China, scaled Mt. Everest and thumbed her way across the desert to get to some place that served milkshakes, she loved the damn things. As I would soon find out, she'd slurp one down, make a trip to the bathroom and be ready to polish off another one. The kid had it bad for the sweet stuff. Too bad there wasn't a milkshake slurping contest I could enter that kid in, she'd win every time.

Chapter 22

Hitting The Bank

The trip to the bank went good. The check got cashed, and the kid walked away with two suckers. Yeah, the teller gave her an extra one for being so cute. Evidently, that had its advantages. God knows I never walked out of the bank getting anything from them for free. I made a mental note to myself to make sure and bring the kid back with me next time I went to get a loan. What, you don't think a guy like me knows how to improve his chances? I'm a detective not an imbecile, a 550 credit score or not that kid would improve my chances by 200 percent minimum.

She had eyes that could warm the coldest of hearts. Trust me, I know talent when I see it, and she had that look down pat. It was just when she opened her mouth and started asking questions that you wished you could get rid of her. If I took her in to see the loan officer with me and the cute look she possessed didn't clinch it for me, I could just unleash her on the poor guy until he couldn't take it any longer. I was fairly certain he'd eventually write the check himself just to get us out of his office.

Just when we were about to leave, Kelsey asked if it was time to grab a milkshake. I said, "hang on a second, I just want to speak to this guy over here for a moment. Come on. He likes kids, I can tell. He probably has a few of his own."

The guy was meticulously dressed, fresh starched shirt, silk suit and tie, the works. There wasn't a wrinkle or a stray pet hair on him anywhere to be found. He didn't have kids, in fact he wasn't even married. From my initial assessment I surmised he never would be, but thirty minutes later I walked out of the bank $1,500 to the good thanks to Mrs. Burke's check and the thousand dollar loan Mr. Reynolds handed me. It turns out he wasn't a kid person either. He couldn't wait to get us out of his office, and Kelsey kept her whining to a minimum, but the second time she accidentally kicked his desk made him bypass all of that formality stuff.

There was no lengthy questionnaire I had to fill out asking about cash flow and assets. I'm pretty damn certain he didn't even bother to check my account balance as he said, "oh, I think we can take care of this in no time." He seemed more concerned about his precious mahogany desk than he did about my credit standing. I know, because there is no way on God's green earth he took the time to pull my credit report.

All I had to do was agree to have the loan set up to automatically draft from my account. That was certainly easy enough. He asked, "what kind of work do you do Mr. Pepperell?" I explained I worked for an investigative firm that also did security work, and then he responded with, "well, I can't think of a better place for us to put our money than in your account." With that he stood asking me to look out for his desk while he stepped out a moment to make the deposit for me. What the hell was I to say other than, "sure." My head was swimming at that point, maybe I should have gone for two grand. Either way my immediate financial situation had changed in an instant.

Mr. Reynolds or Clark as I like to call him left his office, and I looked over at the kid. She now had some little do-hickey in her hand that was sitting next to his nameplate. It was some little guy holding a golf club. It looked as though it was made of pewter. I told her to put it down before she broke the thing as she asked, "what's a tin cup?"

"That's a trophy, now put that back where you got it from before he gets back in here with our milkshake money kid."

She did as I instructed, but that's when I heard those words she spoke rather often, "ah oh." That golfer no longer held the club in his hand, Kelsey held it in hers. I just looked at her as I said, "give me that." I tried to stick the thing back in the little man's hands, but it kept falling back out. Now, Kelsey looked up at me as she asked, "can you fix it?"

"I don't think so. I think this guy's tired of holding that club kid. It was probably made in China. They don't make stuff like they used too." I knew of only one way to fix it in a jiffy, and I was fresh out of superglue. To prevent Clark from seeing it, I stuffed the little silver putter in my coat pocket as the kid said, "I think he's coming back." If she was good for anything it was being a lookout.

When Clark walked back into his office he stated, "well, it looks like we have you all taken care of Mr. Pepperell. Let me know if there is anything else I can do for you."

I immediately stood reaching for Kelsey's hand as I said, "thanks Clark. Well, let's go, and let Mr. Reynolds get back to whatever he was doing."

I was fairly certain I would receive a call from him within the next two or three days asking me to help him locate his missing putter. As we walked out of there I said, "well done kid." I didn't know if it was the coin or her bringing me luck. It's not like I'm superstitious, but I wasn't about to waste it.

Chapter 23

Puzzling Task Of Doing Business

I pulled out my phone as she climbed in the car, and I placed a call to Louie. He was my bookmaker, and I'm not talking printer. The line was busy, that meant he was making money too. You probably think you shouldn't be betting Pepper, it's not healthy. Well there's a lot of things in this world that aren't healthy, but a little risk keeps one feeling the adrenaline rush. Perhaps the best place to do it was someplace other than the bank parking lot though.

Things between me and Louie were friendly. I gave him all my action except for the occasional side bet with Teddy, and Louie laid that action off elsewhere, but kept the vig for himself when I lost. Like I said, we were sort of like friends in a way. So now you know how I managed to pay the bills when business was slow, and my luck was running good. That was also how I remained in the hole when business was good, and luck wasn't holding up.

A quick trip by my cell phone service provider to pay the bill to keep the phone from being disconnected, and it was time to swing by Mr. Burke's place of business. Surveying the area, it didn't take long to locate his car as Kelsey continued asking me a thousand and one questions.

I reached over opening up the glove box to retrieve a small GPS locator which I planned to tag his Mercedes with, and that created a whole string of other questions I really didn't care to answer. "What's that?"

"It's detective stuff kid. Trust me, it's boring and you

wouldn't be interested."

The kid wasn't buying it, I could tell. She watched my every move. I told her to stay put while I stepped out of the car a second to check something out.

She volunteered to help as she asked, "are we on a case now?"

"No. I'm on a case. You're solving something else."

"What?"

I reached back inside the glove box feeling around for a key chain I had placed in there months ago. It had a small Rubik's Cube attached to it, and I had tried for countless hours to put the thing back in order whenever I was bored doing surveillance from inside my car. I figured it would keep Kelsey occupied long enough to allow me to tag Mr. Burke's vehicle. I handed it to the kid saying, "work on this until I get back, and see if you can put all the colors on one side."

She had to ask another question, "it's a toy?"

"It's not a toy, it's a key chain that also happens to be a puzzle. See if you can solve it, and then we'll see about tracking us down a milkshake."

"I don't like puzzles."

"Well you'll like this one, just twist the thing. See?"

"It would be better if it was a toy or something. You know like the kind they give you in a happy meal. Hey, maybe we could get a happy meal."

She was full of ideas. I knew of a Chinese restaurant called Happy Panda, and I was always content with the takeout I got from there. I was downright happy when they didn't overcharge me, but this happy meal thing, I had never heard of. Evidently, the toy was a big part of it, at least in the kid's eyes.

"You like toys, right?"

"Yeah, toys are fun."

"Okay, it's a toy. In fact, I think I got it in a happy meal."

"For real?

"Well, yeah. That's what made me buy the happy meal in the first place."

"But you said it was a puzzle."

"Look, I'm old and my memory's not that good. So, forget what I said. It's a toy. Now solve the damn thing."

"Okay."

Suddenly the mini Rubik's Cube took on an entirely different image in Kelsey's mind. She started twisting it a half dozen different ways before I got out of the car. I heard her say, "this isn't going to be easy," as I closed the door. I turned my attention to the moving surveillance cameras positioned inside the parking garage. I was also fairly certain Mr. Burke's car had an auto alarm. All things considered, I had to agree with the kid's assessment of the situation. I pulled out a cigar gauging the timing of the security camera movement, and I held the tracking locator in my hand as if it were a lighter all while walking in the general direction of Mr. Burke's vehicle.

Placing the tracking device on Mr. Burke's car was standard protocol in my line of work so it took place without a hitch. I was back inside my Ford Fairlane in no time, and Kelsey was still hard at it trying to master the cube of frustration as I called it.

The thing was more jumbled up than it was when I gave it to her. In fact, she was damn close to having not one single matching color on any side. I didn't think that was possible to do either, but she somehow managed a way to twist that thing into total disarray almost effortlessly. As we drove away, I made a slight comment about her progress, or her lack thereof I guess is more like it. "Looks like you have a ways to go kid."

She kept looking down staring at the puzzle toy I had given her, and twisting it a time or two before observing it some more. That's when she said, "this is hard. I have almost one of each color on each side, but I'm not sure how to get this blue square over here on this side. See, I have too many white ones, and this side has too many orange. Maybe I should move this yellow over here."

It was amusing to watch her try to figure the damn thing out. I had tried many times, and never managed to come close to solving it. Her little face looked determined though, I'll give her that. I continued driving to a little place I thought would do us both good, and I was thankful the Rubik's Cube had her attention for the moment. I even had a chance to turn on the radio and listen to something I enjoyed for a change without being interrupted.

Several songs later I heard Kelsey say, "I did it, see." She was quite proud of herself. She had managed to configure the thing in such a way that every side showed one of every color on the cube, no duplicates. That's what the kid was going for right from the start. That's when I informed her she was supposed to put only one color on each side of the cube. She said, "that's not what you said to do."
"Yes it is."
"You said put one of each color on each side. That's what I did, see."
She was still quite proud of her accomplishment. I argued my position with her saying, "I didn't say it exactly like that."
"Well, that's what I heard you say."
"I think I know what I said."

"I don't think so, I had my listening ears on."

"Well I'm saying it now, and those listening ears of yours need to be checked." The truth is I had told her to put one color on each side, and that's what she did, technically. Perhaps I should have said make all sides one color to start with. I didn't know how difficult it was to see to it no side had a duplicate color. I certainly wouldn't want to attempt it, but I knew how challenging it would be to put it back like I had it when I bought it. The kid was meticulous and persistent. She was giving it a valiant effort trying to make each side of the cube one solid color. As I drove down the street she asked, "which way do you think I should turn it?"

"I can't look at that right now kid. I have to keep my eyes on the road."

Traffic was heavy, but I still managed to grab a glance at it out of the corner of my eye. "But, I'd go the other way if I were you."

She paused a second looking at it, but she didn't take my advice. By the time we made it to our next destination, she had managed to manipulate the plastic cube in such a way most of the individual colors were in fact on one side. She actually looked as if she were close to solving the damn thing. A puzzle that had perplexed me to no end, the kid seemed to solve in a less than fifteen minutes. "I'm getting close Pepper, look." I pulled into the parking space, and I looked at her handy work. The kid had in fact done it. "How did you do that?"

"I twisted it like you told me. It's not that hard."

She scrambled it back up as I watched her twist, and turn the thing with her tiny fingers. Then she went to hand it to me saying, "here you do it."

I grabbed the thing and stuffed it back in the glove box saying, "nobody likes a showoff kid. Come on, let's go get a milkshake."

Chapter 24

Music, Milkshakes And Mind Games

Eventually, the kid's wish was fulfilled as we entered Zoe's Place. Kelsey had never been there before, so, she had plenty of questions for me. Most of them centered around the look of the place, and what they had on the menu. The look of the joint was retro, and I liked it. She did too I guess, so maybe we did have something in common. She chose the table, and I grabbed a newspaper.

The jukebox also caught her attention, and as I explained Zoe's served up the best shakes in town, she hit me up for some change to feed the colorful music machine. So, the kid was into music as well. Our tastes in that area didn't exactly coincide, but I never took her for a golden oldies, classic rock, blues fan. Few kids were it seemed. That combination was pretty much reserved for guys my age.

She was more into the bubblegum stuff. The kid liked upbeat tunes for the most part that sounded a measure beyond happy. She played any song she could find with the words happy or sunshine in the title. That's why I was treated to listening to Katrina and the Waves "Walking On Sunshine" three times before we left the place.

Kelsey even sang along to it the second time it played. The lyrics weren't that difficult to grasp, trust me I heard them over and over and over again. She didn't have to tell me she loved that song, but she did anyway. Joking with her I offered up, "For a second there I couldn't tell if you were into it."

"Didn't you hear me singing it? That means I like it."

Clearly, the kid didn't pick-up on sarcasm, but she was entertaining I suppose. As far as her singing talent went, she was going to need voice lessons if she ever hoped to make a go of it on stage, but for a seven year old she wasn't half bad. She was better than me, I guess is what I'm saying. I didn't try my hand at that song even though she encouraged me to sing along with her. It wasn't my kind of tune. Still, it made you tap a foot or a finger when listening to it. Kelsey gathered from that, I liked the song too.

The people seated at the table behind her seemed to get a kick out of listening to us argue over my hidden love for the song. Kelsey almost taunted me as she said, "you like it too and you know it. Everyone likes that song. It's the happiest one ever."

With a blank expression glued to my face I asked her, "do I look happy?"

"You don't look sad. I saw you tapping the table."

"So."

"So, that means you like it."

"That could mean I'm impatient." If anyone could teach her about body language it was me.

She just shook her head no as she looked up at me. Then she blasted it to the world or at least loud enough for those around us to hear her say, "you like it, but you don't want to say it cause it's a girl song."

"That's not true."

"Yes it is."

You know how it went from there, but the kid ended the debate with a challenge of sorts. She said, next time it comes on if you move at all, you like it. It was unbelievable, the kid hadn't made it halfway through elementary school. I had only known her for a few hours, and here she was controlling my every move. To make matters worse, I was going to have to listen to the song for a third time. Locating her Aunt Rhea moved to the top of my priority list. As for that song, all I'm saying is it gets stuck in your head after hearing it three times in one afternoon.

As the kid hummed along to "Don't Worry, Be Happy" I turned to the sports section of the paper. Coming off of two wins followed by a loss to the Tampa Bay Blue Devils things seemed as though they were about to kick into high gear for the Sox. Looking at the current standings as I skimmed over the sports page, I had faith in them to heat up their bats, and bring the season to a close hot on the heels of the New York Yankees. The season itself was nearing its end, and Baltimore was the last team they would play to finish it out.

I had a fresh line of credit thanks to Kelsey, her lucky coin or Mr. Reynolds call it however you wish, and I also had hope the Sox would take it all the way to the world series making me financially better off in the process.

My love for the game was great, there's no doubt about that, and betting against my team was never an option. If I felt they may suffer a loss, I sat the bench or took it right alongside them. That's called being a team player I suppose, and my passion for being a part of it increased three fold with a little money riding on it.

Louie was the guy to get ahold of to be part of the action. As I dialed his number on my cell phone, Kelsey questioned who I was calling. I answered her explaining I was just trying to get in touch with a friend hoping to leave it at that. I glanced at my watch to check the time, and she had to offer her observation at that point saying, "maybe your friend doesn't want to talk to you."

"What's that suppose to mean?"

"Well you keep calling, and no one is answering so maybe they don't like you that much. Either that or they're not at home."

"It's a cell phone, and I'll have you know this guy lives to take my calls."

"Yeah, if you say so. I don't think he likes you."

I just looked at her as our waitress came over to take our order.

"What's not to like?"

"I'm just saying."

At least our waitress found her funny. The kid looked at me, and then she looked up at the waitress attempting to place her order. Kelsey had difficulty deciding between strawberry and banana though. The waitress told her she could have both in one glass. "It's called a side by side shake," she said. That made Kelsey's day. She wasn't bashful about announcing she liked Zoe's Place.

After telling the waitress what we wanted, I turned my attention back to the newspaper. Kelsey eventually offered, "that's okay. I had a friend like that too. Her name was Shelby, and she didn't like to talk much at all."

"Maybe you never gave her a chance."

"What's that suppose to mean?"

"I'm just saying."

Now the waitress found me to be the one with the humorous side as she set our milkshakes down on the table in front of us. That quieted Kelsey down long enough for me to make one more attempt at getting Louie on the phone to place my bets. The final match-up rounding out the season with the Orioles looked promising to me from where I was sitting. Yes, things were looking good for the home team. That's the way I saw it as I sat across the table from Kelsey sucking down a cool one, a milkshake that is.

My flavor of choice was vanilla which the kid claimed was boring just by the sound of it. She branded things quick based on her emotions coupled with limited experience, and she made her determinations sound convincing. So much in fact, I questioned in my mind if she was right, but boring or not I like vanilla. It was my thing, and the most annoying part of it all was how this little girl had the uncanny ability to get inside my head. You'd think detectives are immune to that kind of stuff. Well, they're not.

The kid was on her second shake before I hardly put a dent in mine. Evidently, her favorite flavor was strawberry. Pink suited her I guess. I hate to admit it but she was growing on me a little. Maybe it was the whip cream mustache she was now sporting that I found amusing or maybe it was the tone in her voice when she asked if she could get another refill. Like I said the kid loved milkshakes, and she was hard at work on slurping the thing down too. The determination on her face was admirable. A long sip she took through the straw caused her eyes to widen a little as she looked directly at me saying, "brain-freeze."
My response to that was, "yeah, you better slow down there tiger. You need to pace yourself like me."

She looked at my milkshake eyeing the cherry nestled in the whipped cream on top of it and her eyes followed it as I set it aside leaving it on the empty saucer next to my newspaper. She only paused a moment for her brain to unthaw, and she quickly asked, "are you going to eat that?"

Chapter 25

Angles And Wagers

Still, unable to reach Louie, I was beginning to grow anxious. It was nearing game time, and I wanted in on the action. You know they say patience is a virtue. Well, I was short on that one less than one hour before the throw of the first pitch. I continued reading through the sports scores as I responded to her question about the cherry I had set aside, telling her, "well, I was going to save it for desert." I lowered the newspaper slightly looking over the top of it at her saying, "but I guess you can have it if that's where you were going."

The kid had a smile on her face that widened even more as she said, "yep, that's where I was going."

She snagged it from the saucer, and she made it known she loved cherries as well before making it disappear. I went back to doing my analysis, and she continued slurping away. Hearing the straw fight for every last drop, I said, "I think you've hit rock bottom kid."

That didn't stop her though. The waitress came over and asked if she was ready for another one. She was only joking I think, but Kelsey wasn't as she said, "yes," with a great deal of enthusiasm behind her positive answer.

Before she could complete her order I said, "nice try, but the well is dry kid." I looked over at Janice and said, "two is her limit. We're ready for the check."

Kelsey was already trying to get me to commit to bringing her back the next day, but with less than thirty minutes to game time my attention was focused elsewhere. I said, "sure," just to shut her up. At that point, I'd have probably said sure to anything including taking her to Disney World. Lucky for me it didn't come to that, and Louie picked up the phone on the fifth ring this time. I smiled looking over at the kid as she polished off what was left of her milkshake. "Lou this is Pepper."

"Pepper who," he sarcastically asked. Of all the times for him to choose to joke around about knowing me this one seemed truly fitting after my conversation with Kelsey.

"You know which Pepper, you mean to tell me you know more than one." The kid heard my side of the conversation, but I was fairly certain she had no idea what was taking place with that call.

Louie asked, "what took you so long? The line is about to close you know."

"I know it's close, but you know I like the Sox. Tell you what, how about two-fifty straight-up each of the next four games."

"That's some heavy change Sam. You know something I don't?"

"I know they're going to win."

"You always say that, but this time I hope you're right."

"You've gotta love baseball."

"Well, if you don't something's wrong with you."

"So, we're good."

"I've got you down, next four games two-fifty each. You're lucky I like you Pepper."

"How's that?"

"Are you kidding me, ten minutes to pitch time, I'd have told anyone else coming at me with that kind of action to take a walk or sit the first game out." That was Louie's unique way of telling me he appreciated my business. He ended the call telling me to get off his line so he could lay-off some of his book before the game started.

Chapter 26

Loyal Support For The Red Sox

That evening the kid and I enjoyed watching the Red Sox play on the small ten inch television inside my office. Maybe enjoyed is not exactly the right word to use in order to describe the experience. She criticized everything about it actually, from the antenna that pulled out the top of it which consistently needed adjustment to keep lines from rolling up the screen, and the players from going fuzzy. I was used to it.

The TV belonged to Willard, and it came with the office when I took over the business. I can't begin to tell you how many games I had watched on the thing. I listened to the announcers mostly, and I listened out for that ever-loving sound every true baseball fan longs to hear. That of course, would be the crack of the bat striking the hardball. I seldom had to look up at the screen to know what was going on out on the field.

Picture clarity seldom became an issue for me since I was usually working on solving a case while watching the game. The point was I could say I watched it even if I couldn't see it that well on the screen, and with two hundred and fifty dollars riding on the outcome of that game it brought plenty of excitement my way.

Kelsey wasn't thrilled, to say the least, to be stuck inside my office watching the Sox and the Orioles going head to head. They were playing in Baltimore, and I was hoping for the win, obviously. I also had a busy evening planned work-wise. While the kid complained and alerted me to TV malfunctions, I did what I could from my desk to track down anyone I could find in the city named Rhea Fallon. In addition to that, I tried to add some excitement into the whole experience for the kid by saying, "okay, Big Papi is up next kid. Watch this guy, he's a crusher."

She shoved a small handful of popcorn in her mouth as she asked, "what are you talking about?"

"Big Papi."

"That's his name?"

"No his name is David Ortiz. They just call him that kind of like the way people call me Pepper." She couldn't draw the correlation between his real name and his nickname I guess. That was evident by the look on her face.

"I don't get it. What's he going to crush?"

"The ball if we're lucky. Just watch him. He's liable to send the thing out of the park. If he was at Fenway the big green monster would be in for it."

I left her more confused with my words. The kid and I seldom spoke the same language it seemed. She glanced at the tiny little television set, and she looked directly at me as if I had truly lost it.

She felt the need to educate me saying, "there's no such thing as big green monsters. You do know that, right?"

"That's what they call the scoreboard at Fenway Park kid, but they're not there today."

"Oh, what's the monster thing look like?"

"It's big and it's green, and it has lots of numbers on it."

"That's it?"

"Yeah, pretty much."

"That doesn't sound very scary. There's nothing green on this TV."

"That's because it's black and white."

"You should get it fixed, you could get colors put on it.

That would make it better, and maybe make it bigger too."

"Great suggestions, stick them in the box would you."

"Which box?"

"The suggestion box."

"What's a suggesting?"

"Suggestion," I said firmly. I was tired of repeating myself, tired of talking altogether. This wasn't how I preferred to watch baseball. "Look, there's nothing wrong with that TV. It was working in this office long before I was."

"So, it's really, really old. Huh?" She made it sound like I was ancient or something.

I barked, "hey, there's nothing wrong with old stuff." I became a little defensive I guess.

She came back with, "yeah, except that it's old and nobody wants it."

"Well, if that TV had color you'd be able to see plenty of green out there on that field kid."

"But it doesn't have color does it?

"Just use your imagination. You're a kid that shouldn't be too hard for you." She had found my last nerve and she was standing on it.

"I'm trying, but it looks gray to me. I think the grass is dead. Or is that dirt? It's all gray."

"Trust me, out there it's green though, and Big Papi knows how to put it out of the park."

"If he's really big like that monster thing I don't think he can fit on your TV."

"Very funny, just watch the game, and eat your popcorn."

Kelsey turned her attention back to the television, and I even stopped what I was doing to see Big Papi take the plate. Pitch two he hammered one into left-center. The kid did enjoy that part of the game. With a bit more enthusiasm see looked over her shoulder at me saying, "you're right.

He's really good. I like Big Papi."

"Me too kid." Alright, she almost made me laugh a little with her whimsical remark. It was that combined with a look of transparent innocence on her face. Maybe we had uncovered another piece of common ground. As the next batter approached the batters' box she crunched on her popcorn dropping a few pieces on the floor as she said, "maybe this guy can hit it like Big Papi did. I like saying that."

I went back to work thinking probably not, but me being the positive guy which I am, I just replied, "we can hope, kid." I listened to her spout out anything that came to mind as she continued to munch away. That's when she said, "you could have people call you Big Pepper."

"I don't think so."

"What about Dr. Pepper?"

"Trademarked already. Besides, that would be too much fun for them. How about we stick with Pepper private investigator."

She dug her hand back into her bag of popcorn saying, "okay, but I'll think of something else." That I was sure of, one afternoon together, and she was already trying to rename me something goofy. Who was I to complain? I called her kid most of the time, but I had a reason for that.

Chapter 27

Tracking Subjects

My search for Kelsey's aunt turned up empty, but it was early in the process. Nothing comes easy in this world though. We should all know that by now. Things worth finding usually took a lot of time and hard work. I had my fair share in front of me it seemed.

Mr. Burke's vehicle locater wasn't where I had left it though. It appeared he was on the move to some place other than his house. That meant it was time for me to shift gears and follow him just to see what he was up to. I'd probably help end his marriage in the process.

I didn't think about that piece of the puzzle very much when working a case. I couldn't afford to. If he was being unfaithful to his wife, I wasn't the cause of it just the messenger. Sometimes, that wasn't the case at all though. There are still guys in the world that put in the long hours to move up the ranks in their company to pursue their career goals, and provide for their family. It was possible he could've fallen in that category. I wasn't betting on it though. All my money was on the Red Sox for the time being.

There were countless places Mr. Burke could be heading. The gym, a restaurant or even the grocery store. He could have been in need of some personal time. It wouldn't surprise me in the least if he felt the need to stop off, and have a drink to take the edge off before going home to his wife of nearly twenty years. One thing is certain, I was about to find out what he was up to.

The bad part is I had to miss the end of the game, and drag the kid along with me to do it, but it was my job. I could get the sports scores on the radio to determine whether or not I was up or down. What I was going to do with a seven year old while conducting surveillance, I had yet to figure out. It was going to be a challenge though, I knew that.

I stood up from my chair asking the kid if she needed to use the facilities, and she declined. I tried to encourage her to make the trip down the hall because I knew how long it may take being stuck inside my car once we were in position to monitor Mr. Burke's movements.

She watched me load several pieces of spy-ware in a cardboard box as she asked, "where are we going?"
I continued filling the box with a directional amplified microphone, and some recording equipment telling her, "I don't know exactly, but this little thing will tell us."

The GPS monitor was the last thing to go in the box along with my camera. Kelsey was more interested in what I was putting in the box than the game. I told her to turn-off the television, and she asked if we were going to find out what happened to that dead guy. I replied, "no, we're going to work on a real case." Kelsey stared at the little television unsure of how to cut it off.
"Turn it counter-clockwise," I told her.

She grabbed hold of the wrong knob, but that was okay. She also turned it in the wrong direction. "The other knob, in the other direction." Instructing her on how to do something was more work than me actually walking over there and doing it myself, but she needed to learn, I guess.

If this is what being a parent was like I'm glad I missed out on that adventure, I think. Everyday dealing with a kid could have probably made me a complete basket-case. I now had a newfound respect for people with children. I asked, "you're sure you don't have to go to the bathroom? We're going to be in the car for a while."

"No, I'm okay."

"You don't even want to try."

"You can't try. It doesn't work like that."

"Sure it does."

"No, it doesn't. You can't just go when you don't want to," she informed me.

I didn't have a good feeling about her decision, but what could I do to convince her. I said let's go grab us some hotdogs, and get to work then. She looked out my window saying, "it's dark outside."

"I know. Welcome to the world of a detective kid. We never sleep until the case is solved."

"What about the popcorn?"

"Bring it with you and grab us two drinks out of the frig while you're at it."

"What case are we working on?"

"That's highly confidential."

She just stood there looking at me. "What's that suppose to mean?"

"It means I can't share all the details of the case at this time. Now, get our beverages how bout it."

"But I'm you're partner. Right?"

"Technically, you're my client slash assistant, and tomorrow if you're really up for it I'm going to put you to work straightening up this entire office, but tonight we're on stakeout kid."

"That sounds like a partner to me."

"Bob the janitor empties the trash every Monday, and

Thursday, but that doesn't make him my partner, now does it."

"No. I've never even met him."

"That's because this is Wednesday, and you've only been here nine hours. You mean to tell me you still don't have our drinks yet."

"I'm getting them, jeez."

One hour later I found myself waiting outside a restaurant munching on a chili dog listening to sports scores and answering one question after another thanks to my new partner. Mr. Burke's car was there, but there was no sign of him. In the P.I. business that's what you call an empty tail. He was either carpooling with someone else to do his part in helping to save the planet, or he was smarter than I gave him credit for initially.

The evening was shaping out to be a bust. There was no sign of the subject, and I was no closer to getting what I needed. My only hope was I could find out who was with him once he returned to his car.

Chapter 28

Costly Stop

Kelsey grew tired of staring at the Mercedes. I have to admit it was no thrill for me either. Still, she couldn't have picked a worst time to inform me she had to go. I looked over at her saying, "you've got to be kidding me." She shook her head no. "What about an hour ago when I asked you back at the office?"

"I didn't have to go then."

"And now it's an emergency?"

She stressed her words saying, "now, it's a real emergency."

"Crying Jiminy, let's go."

We got out of the car and she apologized for the call of nature that interrupted our less than noteworthy stakeout effort. "I'm sorry."

"Don't worry about it, just hurry up."

"I will, I promise."

I took her inside the restaurant and the hostess greeted us at the door with a friendly, "good evening, how many are in your party?"

"Just two for now, but someone else may be joining us. Do you have a place where we can wash up?"

She directed us toward the restrooms, and I thanked her steering the kid in that direction as she commented on how nice the restaurant was. It looked expensive, too damned expensive for a guy like me, but I wasn't about to share that with the woman that stood between us and the restrooms at that point.

Kelsey asked if we were going to eat there and I told her, "as soon as hell freezes over," as I shoved her through the door of the ladies room. I looked back toward the window trying to gain a line of sight to Mr. Burke's vehicle, but it was impossible to see from where I was standing. A bit impatient at that point, I offered some words of encouragement to Kelsey through the door. "Hurry up in there. I don't have all night."

Thirty seconds later an older woman dressed to the nines opened the door to the women's room, and she exited giving me a look which expressed her displeasure. There was no explaining myself on that one. I just endured her awkward stare for a split-second. She was undoubtedly a well to do gal with money and manners. From the scornful look she gave me she clearly found me to be beneath her standards, but where I ranked on the social acceptability meter at that moment didn't matter.

All I cared about was locating my subject and getting the kid out of the bathroom before the old lady reported me to the manager. If this was a speedy trip, I sure as hell didn't want to wait out a long one. "Are you done in there?" She opened the door as I looked down at my watch. "Ten minutes, wow. That must be some kind of new world record."

"I told you to stop timing me. It's not nice."

"Well, I was running out of things to do after the first five minutes."

As we hastily walked past the hostess, I looked out the window seeing no sign of the car. The hostess asked if we were ready to be seated, but I pretended I didn't hear her as I proceeded out the front door towing the kid behind me.

Kelsey asked, "what's the matter?"

I looked at the empty space where the Mercedes had sat

which was now being filled by another car saying, "something seems to be missing."

The kid finally noticed what it was asking, "where's the car?"

"That's what I'd like to know. Crap!"

"You sure do say a lot of bad words."

"Well what do you want me to say, zip-a-dee-do-dah?

"It sounds better than crap."

"Don't say that?"

"Why not? You say it."

"I don't say it that much."

"You say it all the time. You say it when you're driving, when you drop something, when I say I have to go to the bathroom. It was one of the first words I heard you say when I first met you."

"Okay, point taken. I say the word a lot, but you don't need to say it."

"You say hell a lot too."

"Really, cause I don't think I say that very often."

"You said it seven times today, I counted."

"Okay, I'll make you a deal. You stop counting all the not-so-good words I say, and I'll stop timing you when you go to the bathroom."

"And you'll stop yelling at me through the door."

"Don't push it."

"What are you going to do about the car?"

"I don't know." It was getting late. Burke was probably headed home to his wife, and I had missed whatever contact he had with his secretary for the evening if that encounter actually took place. Who knows maybe he was having a business dinner. I don't know. I didn't see who he was with, unfortunately.

Kelsey appeared concerned when she asked, "does this mean we lost him?"

"Not exactly. It's alright kid. We'll get him next time."

Chapter 29

Given The Slip

Against my better judgment, in an effort to salvage the time spent tracking Mr. Burke up until that point, I checked the car location using the GPS only to find it was traveling south. He certainly wasn't headed to the gym or to his house. My guess was he was on his way to visit someone Mrs. Burke would not have approved of. This was my chance to end this case quick, and time in every business is money. The faster you can make it the better.

If I missed that opportunity, I may have been stuck tracking him for another week or two. That didn't sound appealing. I looked down at Kelsey as we headed toward my car. "Are you up for a late night kid?"

She responded with, "sure. Where are we going now?"

"We're going to find the guy driving that car, and this time he's not giving us the slip."

The only good news I had at that point was the Red Sox had won, and I was two-hundred and fifty bucks to the good. I was now willing to press my luck even further. Kelsey found the GPS locator to be quite interesting to say the least. "How does it know where the car is?"

"Satellites tell it using coordinates, and it tells us."

"So, it can tell you where to find anything?"

"Sure."

Kelsey tried talking to it as it instructed me to go three miles and turn left. She asked it where the nearest Burger King was, and then she complained it was ignoring her.

"Right now, it's focused on finding the car just like we

should be."

"How does it work, exactly?"

"I don't know. If I did I wouldn't be running down this guy."

"Well, what would you be doing then?"

"I'd be enjoying the good life somewhere other than here. Has anyone ever told you, you ask a lot of questions?"

"Just you."

Almost a minute of silence was experienced as I drove to Mr. Burke's present location. I would eventually find out it was his secretary's apartment. I'm sure he was just there to give her something she had left at the office, or seeing to it she had what she needed to perform her duties at work.

The vehicle was once again found all by its lonesome. Burke must have been inside one of the apartments, but the question remained which one. Kelsey was excited to see the car we had stared at for almost an hour back at the restaurant, but her excitement quickly waned as we gawked at it for another hour.

"Maybe we should be trying to find who killed that dead guy."

"Please stop calling him the dead guy, and that case is pro bono. You know what that means?"

"No."

"That means it doesn't pay anything. It's like a favor."

"Yeah so."

"So, basically, no money means no milkshakes."

"Oh, maybe we should do this, whatever this is."

"It's called working a case, just be patient."

"So, you're getting paid to sit here?"

"That's right."

"You got an easy job. What's the camera for?"

"Pictures."

"I know that. Want to take a picture of me?"

"Not right now."

"Why not?"

"Cause I got work to do kid."

"All you're doing is sitting here."

"No. I'm working, here do a crossword puzzle."

"I don't want to do a crossword puzzle. I want to do something fun. Let's go somewhere else."

"We can't go somewhere else until I'm done here."

"Well can you hurry it up? I don't like this place, it's boring, and your car smells funny."

The kid really knew how to hurt a guy. "Are you always so critical? You know you're never going to make friends that way."

"What's critical?"

"Critical is the case we're on. We have to sit here whether we like it or not."

"How many friends do you have," she enquired.

"It depends on the day of the week kid. Now, try and be quiet. Okay?"

"Okay, I'll try."

No more than ten seconds passed before she asked, "what are their names, you know your friends? I bet they're old like you, aren't they? Hey, am I your only kid friend?"

I just looked at her. The kid had to be getting tired, but she was draining every ounce of energy I had at that very second.

"Hey, I got an idea," she said.

"Yeah, what's that?"

"I can take a picture of you."

"You don't ever give up do you?"

"Can I see it?"

I held the camera up out of the reach of her hands. "See."

"I mean can I hold it."

"That's not what you said. Look kid this is a delicate piece of equipment." She started to reach for the directional microphone and the headset beside her. "So is that. Don't touch, remember."

"How can I be your partner if you don't trust me with your stuff?"

"I trust you."

"You do?"

"I trust that you'll find every word there is in this word find. Here give it a shot."

"I'm hungry. Maybe we should get a pizza."

"What do you want me to do call Dominos?"

Some stakeout this was. I didn't want to bring her along, but what choice did I have. I reached inside the paper bag I had in the front seat next to me. As I pulled out a chili dog I had purchased from the gas station I heard, "are you really going to eat that?"

Looking directly at it I replied, "yes I am. You want some?"

"No way," she said.

I just shrugged my shoulders taking a huge bite, and as it would figure here comes Mr. Burke. I didn't see which apartment he exited, but I was willing to wager it was the one that had the shapely blonde standing at the door. If she was the woman in question from what I saw of her she seemed to have the whole package, and everything was in the right places so to speak.

I could see why Mrs. Burke wasn't fond of her right off the bat. She had legs all the way up to her - well never mind that. I did have a kid in the car. She stood there waiting for Mr. Burke to get something out of his vehicle. I had no doubt he would return to her apartment based on what I could see of her.

Tossing the messy remains of the chilidog down on the sack beside Kelsey she uttered, "yuck," as I fumbled for my camera which I dropped in the floorboard. I leaned down to get it, and my shoulder hit the horn just as Mr. Burke was about to step away from his car. I could see him in the side view mirror as he looked over toward the vehicle not sure of where the horn honk had come from. I remained frozen with my head lowered and my hand gripping the camera.

Kelsey snickered at me. I pulled my pointer finger to my lips hoping to keep her quite, but that just made her break out into full laughter. Evidently, she didn't get the meaning of the hand gesture. I know I must have sounded like Elmer Fudd when I whispered, "we have to be very, very quiet." God you would have thought someone told her the funniest joke in the world. That's when her laughter really erupted.

Fortunately, Mr. Burke had already turned his attention to his secretary's apartment. Watching him turn walking toward her door, I quickly popped my head up, and snapped a shot of him as he surveyed the rest of the parking lot on his way to meet her. "You're funny Pepper."
"Why are you taking pictures of him?"
"Cause he's the job kid."
"Who's she?"

The kid never ran out of questions. I could have used her grilling a suspect, and I'm certain she would have broken them. Hell, she was breaking me. "Circle the words, kid." "What's S.E.R.E.N.D.I.P.I.T.Y spell?" Unable to get a clear shot of both him, and his secretary, I may have uttered a four letter word that started with "S". I'm still not sure on that, but the kid replied, "no that's not it. I know how to spell that, and that's a bad word."

I looked over at Kelsey asking, "what do I look like, a dictionary."

"I just asked, if you don't know how to spell just say so."

"What's the word?"

She labored to spell it again. I looked back at the apartment as I said, "serendipity kid. That's what I live by."

"I thought you said you live by the seat of your pants."

"I live by a lot of things, same difference."

"Oh." She then latched on to that word, and she kept repeating it over and over and over, you get the point. All I know is the kid really liked that word kind of the same way she liked the name Big Papi. I don't think I would have made it without the headphones. I put them on, and picked up the directional mic plugging it into the recorder. Suddenly, she became interested in what I was doing. Nothing else seemed to matter. "What are you doing now?"

"I'm trying to listen. You should do the same."

"Are you spying on them?"

"It's not spying. It's called surveillance."

"You're spying. Can you really hear what they're saying?"

I gave her a look as I said, "I can when it's quiet."

"Oh, sorry," she whispered back.

Chapter 30

Intricacies Of Sex And Espionage

The kid was actually quiet for several minutes. I was able to pick-up some chatter inside the apartment, and from what little I heard it was apparent Mr. Burke was dabbling where he shouldn't. His secretary had quite a mouth on her. From what I heard her say through the headphones, she could probably make a sailor blush. I should know, I used to be one, and my ears were a little warm at that moment. I assure you the heat I felt wasn't coming from the headphones. It was coming through them. It was the way that woman talked that could get a guy excited, not to mention what she could dangle in front of him.

I have to say Mr. Burke knew how to pick them. There were times in my life where I would have... That's when my train of thought was interrupted by a voice that was not my own. Kelsey asked, "what are they doing?"

Instinctively, I responded, "Oh, I think we know what they're doing..." I stopped myself short of saying another word as I looked over at the seven year old seated beside me.

"Well, what?"

I wasn't about to scar her for life. I'd leave that to the rest of the world because the world itself is pretty damn good at it all on its own.

"Probably playing a game of some sort."

"Like what?"

"Poker, scrabble, tiddlywinks, take your pick."

"I don't like any of those games. Tiddlywinks is stupid."

"Yeah. Well give it time kid, they may grow on you."

"I don't think they're playing a game. I bet they're doing it."

Where the hell did that come from? I was more caught off guard than a blind third baseman with a lefty up at bat. I didn't know what to say to her. So, I chose to ignore it. You know the rule ignore it and it goes away. Right? Guys live by that rule. It's ingrained in every fiber of our being, an inherent survival mechanism I employ whenever needed, and it works. Evidently, that doesn't apply to awkward conversations, and little girls.

Kelsey looked over at the half eaten chili dog, and then she glanced over at my lap. She then proceeded to scar me for life by asking, "so, is that what they call it, a wiener?"

On that note, I removed the headphones and unplugged the microphone as I looked at her. She turned her attention back to the word find puzzle circling another word. I wasn't about to get roped into telling her all about the birds and the bees. I was still trying to figure a few things out for myself. All I said was, "they're not doing it."

"Well, I bet they're going to."

I had already been down this road before, and Kelsey knew how to badger you to the point of saying something you shouldn't. At least she made you feel as though you shouldn't have said something regardless of what it was or the circumstances. She had this stubborn, feisty way about her that would drive you crazy at times. Oh, let's just face it, she was a woman trapped inside the body of a seven year old. "Look, I'm going to level with you kid." She was listening, I could tell because her pen stopped moving in the middle of circling a word. "This stays between you and me, no one else can know this. That guy you saw entering that apartment, he works for our government. He has high level security clearance."

"What's that mean?"

"That means he knows stuff the rest of us don't."

"What kind of stuff."

"Important stuff, stick with me kid. Somehow, he has a connection to the woman you saw."

"Who is she?"

"Well, we can't be certain until the facial recognition is done, but sources close to me believe that she is Natasha Levkov, a beautiful Russian operative sent here to gather intel about our nation's defense plans, and it's my job to determine if she is attempting to purchase top secret information."

"I knew it," she said.

"That's right this is big, but you have to keep a lid on it."

"Are you going to arrest them?"

"No. I'll leave that to the FBI. I just need to get a few photos of them together as proof they met, and record some of their communication, then we can go get that pizza."

I know what you're thinking, way to go Pepper, lie to the kid. Some great role model you are. Well it worked, and I didn't have to explain how babies are made to her. Slice it any way you want, that's a win in my book. It took longer than I anticipated, but I was ready when Mr. Burke's secretary opened the door for him to leave. I grabbed a quick snapshot of them standing just inside the door with her arm casually hanging onto his shoulder.

In this business, that's called the money shot. Divorce attorneys, and their clients pay big bucks for it. Mr. Burke had no idea what he was in for, I did though. It wasn't going to be pretty. Reflecting back on his wife's words, I thought maybe he had given his wife the best years of his life, and in a moment of weakness made a poor choice all because something was missing in his world. That list of motivations could be miles long. It's hard to hang onto some things in a seventeen year marriage - passion, excitement, and sex are usually the first things out the door.

That aside, I'd have put my money on one reason Mr. Burke cheated. Like any man his age, it's hard to overcome what is felt when given the attention he was being handed from an attractive young woman. Then again, maybe he was the kind of guy that could never be faithful since the day he got married, and in his later years got sloppy and gave up caring. Either way I try not to judge people, especially when I don't know all the circumstances involved in their decisions.

The one fact I do know is we're all human, and you know what comes with that. A sizable numbers of mistakes made throughout the course of our lives and some of them carry more weight than others. My job was to discover the truth no matter what the outcome was. It was unfortunate though, seventeen years of marriage gone in the flash of a snapshot. I don't know what caused his recent infidelity. It wasn't my place to figure it out. I did what I was hired to do. I just didn't look forward to sharing the information with Mrs. Burke, but it had to be done.

Still, I didn't gain a great deal of satisfaction working cases where someone was cheating on their spouse, but it was a big part of this business. Avoid those cases, and like my old mentor Willard Derkin used to say, you better get used to skipping a few meals. I found him to be right about that, and I learned quick to never turn down the easy bucks.

I placed the camera in the seat next to me, and I looked up adjusting my rear view mirror. I could see Kelsey stretched out in the backseat with my coat covering her to keep her warm. The kid was out cold. She looked innocent lying there not making a sound. I made a note of the time as Mr. Burke got in his car, and drove away. Then, I cranked up my car and turned the heater on to drive out the chill. Kelsey didn't budge as I pulled out of the parking lot.

Knowing the bulk of the work in the Burke case was done except for developing a few photos, and retrieving the GPS locator, I questioned at that point what I was going to do with the little girl in the backseat. I mean, it's not like I had any place for her to sleep. Two months with little business, and slow paying customers to boot, put me in a bit of a tight spot, my office was now my apartment. I told myself it was temporary at the time, but temporary turned into five months. I had actually become accustomed to living in a cracker box and the work commute was now non-existent. Truthfully, it had just about everything I needed, including a microwave and a small refrigerator. I even managed to shower at the Y down the street from my office, and I usually sleep on the sofa when I wasn't stuck sitting inside my car until the wee hours of the morning.

Maybe my job wasn't quite as easy as the kid thought. There were plenty of things about this line of work she had no business knowing. I just knew sleeping in the car wasn't an option, not for her at least. It was cold that time of year and far from safe. My living situation was fine for me, but not a kid. I didn't know much about caring for one, but I was determined to keep her safe. As I drove, I began to doubt I had what it took to care for her, but then it struck me. Hell, if I couldn't keep the kid safe, who could. Suddenly, I felt like I had what it took to pull it off.

I'm still no babysitter mind you. So, don't try to hire me to watch your kids for the weekend while you're out of town cause, I won't take the job. I mean it - not unless things are really, really slow, they're potty trained, and they know how to dress themselves. Excuse the digression.

Parking the car next to the curb in front of my office, I told myself nothing would come before finding Kelsey's aunt now that the Burke case was essentially done. That's when she woke up. I could hear her yawn as she rolled over in the backseat. "We're here kid."

"Where are we?"

"Right now the place I call home."

"Did you get your pictures of Natasha?"

"Natasha… Oh, yeah. We got them." Kelsey squinted as she looked out the window, it was dark, but the street lamp put plenty of light on the sidewalk.

"This looks like your office."

"Yeah, it does. Funny story about that actually, but I'll tell you later. Right now, let's get you out of the cold."

I opened her door, and she threw her arms over my shoulders as I picked her up. I grabbed my coat covering her back, and I closed the door with my foot. The kid must have been exhausted, she felt like dead weight as I carried her up the stairs, but something about it was - I don't know… pleasant I guess is the right word. I'm not sure, don't have an occasion to use that word too much. Anyway back to the story, focus people.

Standing at the door, I fumbled in my pocket for the keys to my office as I held her in my arm. Once inside, I placed her on the sofa, and covered her up. It wasn't much, I know, but that office was all I had. "You need to use the potty kid?" She shook her head no with her eyes still closed as she snuggled up on the sofa. I didn't know if she heard me or not but I said, "I'll be in the next room, if you need me you come get me."

Just when I turned to walk away I heard her say, "good-night, Pepper."

I stopped there at the door. I didn't bother to look back over my shoulder at her. I had something in my eye at that moment. No, it's not what you're thinking. Come on, I'm a gritty detective with a mean streak a mile wide when it's called for. You think some sweet little girl is going to get to me, you're wrong. Those that know me know I play for keeps, and all that stuff. Just so we're straight about it, she's just a case like any other. That's what I told myself as I stood there motionless.

Now that we're on the same page so to speak, I'll admit it wasn't often someone said good-night to me. Kind of reminded me of that TV show *The Waltons* in a way cause that's the only place I remember those words being spoken. I just said, "good-night kid, see you in the morning." I then made my way over to my desk, took a seat in my chair, and propped my feet up as I watched her through the open doorway from the other room inside my office. It was time to get a little shuteye myself since it was already morning at that point. The previous day had been a long one. I was tired, and beat, the kid had worn me out, but still I couldn't rest without doing some self-perspective. You don't think I'm going to share those thoughts with you do you? Forget about it, that's personal.

Chapter 31

An Unexpected Call

The sun came up at a few minutes after seven, and it wasted no time finding my eyelids as the bright light entered through the window in my office. I woke to the sound of my own snore. It was cut short though, and suddenly everything was quiet. My feet were right where I had left them, propped up on my desk, and I remained reclined in my chair as I struggled to keep my eyes closed. My winter scarf was still draped over my shoulder, and the loose end of it dangled near the floor. I reached down grabbing it, and I tossed it over my eyes, and forehead in an effort to block out the sunlight. I just wanted one more hour of sleep, that's all. I thought to myself, is that really too much to ask for. Little did I know, that question would be answered soon enough in the form of a phone call.

Taking my left hand, I pinched the edge of my scarf between my thumb and forefinger. Cracking one eye, lifting the edge of the scarf, I checked to see if the little girl was real or if I dreamed her up. She was still sacked out on the sofa where I left her. So, it was confirmed, I did receive a kid in the mail, talk about your special deliveries. Right about the time I drifted back to sleep, the phone rang. A bit caught off guard, I just about fell out of my chair as my feet came flying off the desk, one of them landing in the wastebasket. I only had two thoughts at that moment, first and foremost was don't wake the kid. I was serious about that, as I fumbled to get to the phone which was now hanging on by a thread to the edge of my desk. The other thought I had was, who in the hell could this be calling at that hour.

I picked up the phone on the next ring as I looked into the other room to see if the kid was still asleep. For a moment, I was frozen, hunched over my desk like some kind of private eye wax figure. That's when I heard a voice from the past coming through the phone receiver, a guy I hadn't spoken to in over three years. You guessed it, it was Eddie Fallon. "Pepper, are you there? Hey. Talk to me, this is Eddie."

I knew who it was by the time he uttered the word there. I just couldn't believe he was calling, but I had a question or two for him. "What's the big idea Eddie?"

"Hey, there you are. I was calling to see if you got what I sent you?"

"Yeah, I got it alright. She's sleeping on my sofa as I speak."

"Ah, that's great."

"No it's not. Like I said, what's the big idea?"

"Hey, you said if I ever needed anything just let you know if you could ever do something for me. Well, I need something Pepper."

"You need to have your head examined."

"No. I need a favor, and you offered to help."

"First of all, a favor falls more along the lines of grab me a sandwich while you're out, not here take care of the kid, sign here."

"Hey look, you said…"

"I know what I said, I was just being polite. Don't you understand meaningless remarks when you hear someone say them?"

"No, you meant it. I could tell by the sound of your voice."

"Oh, so now you're a voice expert like me."

"Maybe so, but face it Pepper, deep down inside you care about people. That's why I sent Kelsey to you."

"Look, I don't know the first thing about taking care of a

little girl. I'm the last person you should have sent her to."

"No, you're the first. If anyone can find Rhea that would be you."

"You mean the aunt she's never even seen?"

"Yeah, she's my little sister. She'll take care of her, all you have to do is find her. Last I heard she moved to Massachusetts."

"Yeah, well how long ago was that?"

"Awe, probably about the time I did my first stretch." Guys like Eddie didn't talk in years, they talked in terms of time spent in the clink. Years were too painful to think about, much less mention out loud, speaking of them reminded them of how much of their life had slipped away resulting from a bad decision they made. It was just easier to say my time in the can, but the guys doing the time avoided calling it what it was at all cost unless they were deadly serious.

I knew when Eddie did his first stretch, I'd read his record, and if my eidetic memory served me correct that was close to ten years ago. I knew Eddie's prison record almost as well as he did. Evidently, he wasn't much on keeping in touch with family. I wouldn't be either under those conditions. Considering how much time he spent in the joint instead of on the outside, it was best I guess. Eddie realized that, and he shielded his family from it. He didn't want them to see him behind bars, he didn't like the way he looked wearing white and orange. As I would find out, truth was, he didn't want the women in his life to worry about him. That included his mother, his sisters and his niece, Kelsey, and that's why she knew nothing factual about Eddie other than his name. Everything she was ever told about him was a lie. Eddie lived behind them his whole life. He was comfortable there, he depended on them. Lies we tell can oftentimes become our own prison, but without them he'd have been lost. I knew that, I even understood it.

We all have things we choose to use as fronts, Eddie was just a master at distorting the truth in such a way you believed him. He had you wanting to believe him and the unique ability to gain your trust using both logic and guilt. At that point in the conversation, I was grumbling about the situation Eddie had put me in, and I was trying to gain what I needed to find his sister, but reality was I was just glad Aunt Rhea was real, not just some fictitious person he created out of necessity. Eddie had a knack for it like I said.

The last thing I needed was a kid in my life, you know that. I'm a private eye, and on the mean streets of Boston, I can't go running and gunning with a little girl tagging along behind me. Venting some I said, "you do know, there's probably some kind of law against shipping kids to people that don't know them."

"I'm not sure about that, but I didn't have a choice. I'm counting on you to find my sister, and deliver Kelsey to her. Promise me you'll do it, and I'll see to it you're paid for your trouble."

I looked over at the kid. She was still asleep. I liked her when she was napping, maybe I just appreciated the quiet. I don't know. I knew I didn't like making promises, not to anyone. I learned a long time ago on some, you just can't deliver. Since then, I tried to steer clear of making them, but Eddie had a way of pushing you. I guess Kelsey picked up that trait from her uncle. Talk to either one of them long enough, and you found yourself doing exactly what they asked you to.

Eddie reminded me where he was as he said, "look, I can't talk long my phone time is almost up. Sorry about waking you by the way. Give Kelsey a hug for me."

I had more questions as I asked, "do you have a last address? Do you think her last name is still Fallon, and what's the story with her mother?"

Eddie quickly spouted, "Kelsey's mom died when she was three, that's when my mom started taking care of her. Kelsey never met her father, and I don't think she remembers much about Shannon."

Shannon was Eddie's big sister, she had a thing for men, and she went through lots of them according to Eddie. It was no wonder that Kelsey had never met her father, Shannon would have had a hard time figuring out which one was responsible for getting her pregnant. She died in a car accident while Eddie's mother was watching Kelsey. The kid remained in her grandmother's care ever since, up until a little over a week ago.

Eddie didn't like talking about Shannon or his mother very much, both subjects were uncomfortable for him. His mother took things hard after losing her eldest daughter, and Eddie wasn't about to let her in on the fact that he was doing another stretch in prison. What was so amazing was he was able to keep it from her, and still make sure she received the money she needed to help take care of Kelsey. How do you accomplish something like that while being housed in the federal pen? Well, you'd have to ask Eddie Fallon. Seeing as we were talking on a phone inside the prison, I didn't feel the need to go into that. I can tell you Eddie had his own address outside the penitentiary. That's where he sent and received all of his mail from. A place called Mail Boxes R' Us was where he set up shop to keep his mother unaware of his present location. Eddie explained she was suffering from early onset dementia. A neighbor had contacted social services when Eddie's mother no longer recognized her granddaughter. A call was placed to an answering service Eddie had employed to field all of his calls from his mother, and anyone else that tried to reach him by phone.

As far as I know, I may have been the only person that knew about his stretch in the big house other than those there, and of course, the FBI itself along with Ernesto Salazar. He sounded more like a drug runner than con man, maybe he was. Eddie had a way of hooking up with the wrong people. Choosing me to help him was the best move he ever made. You know what they say, even a blind squirrel finds a nut sometime. Yeah, I was the nut in that analogy. That fit, the kid drove me crazy, and I was nuts for trying to help Eddie in the first place. Anyway, I knew my time was getting short as I heard the guard in the background give Eddie a time warning saying, "one minute." Eddie said, "I don't know if Rhea is married or not. Mom hasn't talked to her in years. I was going to try and find her myself, but the warden restricted my internet use, said something about me being a security risk. I don't know."

"Yeah, well I know."

"Hey, I swear I wasn't up to nothing."

That of course meant he was up to something. Eddie knew how to properly use a double negative. He was no dummy.

"How did you manage to keep her from going to child services?"

"Easy, I just filled out a few forms, and sent them to the right people. You know me Pepper."

"Yeah, I know you pretty well."

Eddie continued with, "yeah, I'm glad we met each other. Otherwise, I'd have been screwed. So, I returned the call routing it through my answering service, and I talked to the social worker myself, told her I was Kelsey's uncle, and I'd see to it she was taken care of, then I made arrangements to purchase the plane ticket, and have her transported to the airport."

"That's how she ended up at my office, air freight express?"

"That's right you got it."

Looking at the special delivery lying on my sofa I said, "yes, I certainly do."

That's when I heard the guard say, "times up."

I expected to hear the phone click followed by a dial tone, but this was Eddie Fallon on the other end of the line. What did I tell you about Eddie? You talk to him long enough, you'd do anything he wanted you to. That was true about Eddie and this proves it.

Eddie said, "hang on, just a second. I only need one more minute, this is important."

He wasn't talking to me, he was talking to the guard. Eddie was bold, you had to give that to him. The guard barked back with, "I don't care, I said time is up."

Eddie responded with, "I said it's important, a little girl's life depends on it."

I didn't expect to hear what I heard next, but to my amazement the guard firmly stated, "okay, but just one more minute."

Eddie had a way about him, I'll admit it. He spoke to me as he said, "Pepper look, I know there's nothing I can do for her in here. I just want what's best for the kid, and that's to be with what family she's got. You understand that don't you?"

"I understand what you're asking me to do is a long shot."

Eddie cut me off, he didn't want to hear the rest of what I had to say. I wouldn't either if I were sitting with my hands cuffed. "All I know is she's my niece, my big sister's baby girl. I haven't seen her since she was three years old, but mom sent me plenty of pictures of her. She's cute isn't she."

What do you say to someone in a situation like that? I mean, Eddie cared about her, and sure she was cute, I guess. Alright she was adorable at times even when she was busting my chops about something insignificant. "I just said, "sure. I guess if you like kids and all."

Eddie chided back with, "you better watch out, she'll break your heart Pepper. I know, she looks just like her mom did when she was little."

"Well, at least she didn't take after you in the looks department."

"Find Rhea. You said call you if I needed something, well I'm calling, and you know what I need."

"I can't promise anything Eddie."

"Are you going to help me or not? I need you on this one Pepper."

"You know how hard it is to find people that family hasn't seen in ten years? Those are people that don't want to be found."

"Name your price."

"This could get expensive. What are you making a buck fifty an hour pressing out license plates in the metal shop? How are you going to pay me?"

"It's seven bucks a day, three days a week and it's all tax free, but don't worry I have a little something working on the side."

He started to elaborate about his side business, but right then I stopped Eddie from saying anything else. That's the thing about him that got him in trouble, he never managed to keep his mouth closed when he talked to someone he trusted. "Wait a minute, I don't want to know. Forget I asked in the first place." I knew, the less I knew about where Eddie's money was coming from the better. As for

Eddie's tax free money he made stamping plates went, Eddie never paid taxes on the money he made when he was a free man. There was certainly no reason for him to start paying them now while he was behind bars. That's what went through my mind, but that thought was interrupted by Eddie saying, "don't worry, I'll get you your money."

There was no telling what Eddie had going. I was just hoping he didn't get caught. So far his track record wasn't looking so hot. I heard the guard say, "times up," and then I heard Eddie say, "just one more minute." That part was humorous as long as he didn't get his skull cracked, but in Eddie Fallon fashion he amazed me once again saying, "I'll do whatever it takes to see to it she has a good life, Pepper. I mean that. The kid's been through a lot. She needs something good to happen to her. I'm hoping that's Rhea, but I'm not about to let her fall into the system. I know what happens to kids that don't have someone to look out for them."

"Yeah, they end up right where you are or worse."

"That's right, and I'm not about to let that happen to her. I'll draft my own pardon and sign the damn thing if that's what it takes to get out of here, and do what I have to do for her." Eddie didn't have to add, "and I'm not joking here. I mean it Pepper, you tell me you'll take care of her until you find Rhea. I trust you."

I knew he wasn't joking. Eddie was the only guy I had ever met that was bold enough, smart enough, yet stupid enough along with skilled enough to pull off what he just said over a prison phone line, which was probably being monitored at that very moment. All I said was, "I didn't hear a word of that, and I'll do it Eddie. I promise you."

That's right, Pepper broke rule three yet again, don't make

promises to your clients. It was more of Willard's rule than mine. Looking back at the Jennings case, and now this one, I seemed to consistently break it. Mostly cause people needed to hear it from me to continue going on. Eddie needed to hear it before he did something crazy. I needed to say it cause like it or not Eddie Fallon was now a friend for putting that kind of trust in me. A lot of things can be done on faith, Eddie reminded me of that during our ten minute conversation that should have ended in five. Thanks to a guard with a soft spot and a convict with a persuasive nature, I got some needed information at 7:45 in the morning. When the guard finally said, "time," this time he meant it.

Eddie said, "I gotta go. It was good talking to you Pepper."

"Hang in there, I'll take care of her."

All I heard after that was Eddie's voice say, "I knew I could count on you," and the click I expected to hear five minutes earlier followed by the dial tone.

Chapter 32

Don't Be Judgmental

What do you want me to say? I had a kid on my sofa that needed someone to care for her, and that person was over three hundred and fifty miles away doing life behind bars. It wasn't right, welcome to my world. Did I care? You're damn right I did. I made a promise, and that was important to Eddie. He knew once I made it, I'd do what I set out to do regardless of the costs. Out of all the things about me, whenever I looked in the mirror which wasn't often, that was the one thing I liked about myself. It certainly wasn't the gray hairs I seemed to collect, but I always kept my word. Everyone that knew me knew that. Making that promise often made me a better detective, it damn sure made me determined. This time, I had to make it payoff for the kid's sake and Eddie's.

He had watched his niece grow up in photographs, even though he wasn't an active part of her life in person. He sent her things though, birthday cards, Christmas gifts, and money to help his mom out raising her. I liked Eddie, but I gained new respect for him that morning. His words stuck with me, especially the part where he said, "she's family, and she's not going to grow up in foster homes." Criminal or not I admired him for doing what he believed was right when it came to the kid. For a guy with financial motives woven into the very fiber of his soul, you couldn't tell it when it came to Kelsey. I was now able to see another side of Eddie through that experience, and I liked it.

I know it sounds cliché, but family came first in Eddie's

world. That's why his mother wasn't stuck in some state run facility with substandard care. Eddie saw to it she had the best of everything including a private room in one of the nicest nursing care facilities in upstate New York. A private room was something Eddie didn't have where he was at for the moment, but I'm certain he would have paid for the upgrade himself given the opportunity. Either way he understood the value of it, and he took care of his mother as best he could from where he was sitting, and no, I didn't ask where he got the money. It was none of my business.

You may say that's not how a detective operates. A great detective has to know everything. Well maybe you're right but as far as I was concerned, Eddie did what any good son would do for his mother under those circumstances, and I tended to cut him a little slack for the effort shown on his part. I thought I knew everything there was to know about Eddie Fallon from my meeting with him in person, and his rap sheet along with a few letters he sent me. Little did I know, Eddie was a master of disguise when it came to keeping his most recent felony convictions secret from his mother. She was now sixty-eight, and she had Rhea late in life. Eddie was just a few years ahead of his sister, and several years behind Shannon. On the phone I had said, "you put a lot of faith in me for a guy who's still behind bars, you know."
Eddie's response to that was, "that's not your fault Pepper."

He was right, it wasn't my fault. He had accepted responsibly for what he had done, but I couldn't keep my wheels from turning. Eddie got a raw deal, and I knew it. Ernesto Salazar had eluded the FBI and played Eddie like an old tune he knew by heart, but outwitting me was another story. I had one advantage Eddie didn't, and that was Ernesto didn't know me. That, combined with the skills and contacts I had acquired in this business, and me being on the outside gave me considerable reach Eddie didn't have. You probably want to know what hit me as I sat back down in my chair to try to grab me another wink. Well, I'll share that with you later. For now, I had to focus on finding Kelsey's aunt.

Trying not to make any noise, I closed my eyes, and raised my feet up, placing them back on my desk. Leaning back in my chair I heard it creak just once. That's when I heard the voice of the kid coming from the other room as she said, "Pepper, I gotta go."

So much for the extra wink, I didn't need it. I was already so damn good looking I couldn't stand it. "Alright kid, I'm coming."

This day was off to a great start I tell you. Returning from the bathroom ten minutes later, Kelsey asked, "what's for breakfast?"

I just looked at her saying, "I don't know."

I had half a pack of bologna, a couple of pieces of cheese, and some coke in the small refrigerator next to the coffee pot. The kid managed to find an old box of dry cereal in the cabinet under the microwave. Hell, I'd forgotten it was even there, leave it to her to find it. I'm telling you the kid was resourceful.

Kelsey said, "I know how to make this."

My reply was, "great, go for it."

Evidently, that was entertaining in some way. She said, "you don't sound at all like Tony the tiger."

I responded with, "that's cause I'm not. I'm Pepper remember."

The kid threw one word at me which was, "boring," and she stretched it out to make her point. I got it alright, the kid had an active imagination. As I walked into the other room I heard her say, "hey, there's no tiger on this box. Where's Tony?" She made it sound as though someone made off with the colorful tiger on the Frosted Flakes box.

I lifted up some papers searching for my coffee mug as I said, "I don't know. I haven't seen him lately."

She came walking into the other room holding the cereal box in both hands interrogating me asking, "what kind of cereal is this?"

It was the cheap kind, the only kind I buy, the kind without sugar. I looked at it saying, "the good kind."

"The kind that tastes good or the kind that's good for you?"

She was upset there wasn't a tiger on the box, like somehow that made it taste better. "Just eat it, you'll like it," I said.

She fired back with, "it doesn't look good."

"Of course it's good, I eat it all the time."

I lied. I hadn't seen that box in months. If I had, it wouldn't have been there in the first place. Needless to say, the expiration date on the top of the box had long passed, but it was cereal. That stuff never goes bad, everyone knows that. Right? The kid didn't trust me on the fact that it was good, I could tell. So, I had to prove it to her. Finding my coffee mug I picked it up, and I held it in my hand as I said, "pour me some, I'll eat it."

She walked over to me and she began pouring it in my coffee mug. Quite a bit landed on my desk, and some actually made it in the cup. That's when I heard her utter, "ah-oh." She looked up at me saying, "I can clean that up."

"Don't worry, I'll get it," I told her. I wasn't mad, there was no harm done, and the kid actually did what I said do. I just didn't specify where to pour the cereal. Now, came the fun part, what to pour over it. I had a choice between bourbon, water or coke. Yeah, I didn't really think this one through, you can tell. The kid asked, "where's the milk?"

"I don't drink milk."

"Why not?"

"Because, I'm lactose intolerant."

"What's that?"

"Don't worry it's not contagious. It just means my stomach doesn't like milk, that's all."

"But milk's good for you though."

"Don't believe the hype kid."

"What do you put on it?"

"Here hand me one of those."

I opened the can of coke and poured a little in my coffee mug then I handed the can back to Kelsey. "This stuff has everything in it you need to start the day off including the sugar. You should have some."

She just stared at me, and her lip curled a little as she watched me prepare to take a sip of the cereal from my coffee mug. Chugging it down in one long gulp, I finished it off sitting my mug down on the table next to the microwave. I made that refreshing sound like they do on the ice tea commercials, and looked at her saying, "now that really hits the spot."

She shook her head and then she asked, "you want some more?"

"Oh, no. I'm good. Don't want to start the day off too full."

Kelsey opted for a piece of cheese, and the rest of the coke I had opened for her. Hey, the kid was smart. She was convinced if there was a tiger on the box it would taste better. So, I told her to draw one. You would have thought I was the most brilliant guy on the planet with that suggestion based on Kelsey's expression. She thought that was a great idea, and she gave me her best impersonation of the cartoon tiger she drew. Then she wanted me to do it, then she wanted me to help her draw the tiger better. I said, "I don't have time for that kid, I've got to find your aunt. Don't you get it?"

She put down the box of cereal she poked several holes in, and she muttered, "it was a dumb idea anyway."

I looked up placing both elbows on my desk, and I looked at her. I had no clue what to say, but I knew something needed saying. It was time to break rule number two: never say you're sorry. I said, "hey kid, I don't say this unless I mean it. I'm sorry. Let me see that cereal box." All I could think is Eddie was right about her. She could break your heart, not mine of course, cause I'm made of steel, and my heart hadn't been used in so long it was completely rusted shut. That's part of what went into making me bulletproof, but the rest of the world... Well, they were in trouble. The rest of the morning was spent doing what Kelsey wanted for a change. I knew she needed her aunt, but right now she needed something else, someone to spend time with her. Searching through directory listings and public records to find her aunt could wait another day it seemed. That day was Kelsey's day pretty much, a trip to the park and to get a milkshake, of course. All I can tell you is it was GREAT!

Chapter 33

Rhea Fallon And Mrs. Grayson

Rhea Fallon was hard to find. Background searches on the internet had turned up lots of records to comb through with few looking as though they would help lead me to her. It was a slow tedious process, city by city, state by state. Now you know why I never cared for missing person cases to begin with if they had been out of touch with family and friends for more than five or six years.

In Rhea's case, it appeared as though she had up and vanished. I felt it was highly likely her name had been changed, and I had my doubts she was still in New York or Massachusetts. Whatever life she started for herself it was hidden to those that once knew her. To find her it was going to take some actual legwork - that meant interviewing former landlords and neighbors. It was a goose chase from the word go, but I had to start somewhere. I made a promise to Eddie, and myself that I would find her.

My hope at that point was it wouldn't be in a cemetery somewhere. What I'd do with the kid at that point, I didn't know. Probably find her a good boarding school for girls, I suppose. At least it was better than foster homes. I should know, I spent time in one, but that stays between us. No one else needs to know. I will tell you the reason I seldom called Kelsey by name, and stuck with the word kid whenever I spoke or referred to her. You learn to avoid personal attachment to things, and people if you don't place specific labels on them. Willard was the same way. He made it clear to me the first day I walked into what is now my office, that he had no intention of growing fond of me, not until I was able to prove myself. I believe his words were, "if you earn your keep, I'll keep you around, and maybe teach you a thing or two." I understood exactly where he was coming from, and that's why we got along so well I imagine. Other than our shared perspective on life, and our passion for working a case, we initially had little in common except for our interest in baseball. That changed with time.

As for the Boston Red Sox, they were winning and the kid, and I were rooting for them right along with Teddy, Joe and Cheeseburger. The dog was wearing a team jersey Joe had bought for him off of e-bay when we went to visit them for lunch that afternoon. All the dog needed now was a shave and some red and white face-paint to look like one of those crazed die-hard fans you'd sometimes see in the stands at Fenway. Either way, Cheeseburger's support for the team probably added an element of fun to the age old sport of baseball, and encouraged the kid to show her love for the game as well.

Joe had to bring up the Grayson case I had mentioned the day before, even though he had no idea what the client's name was. He referred to it as the "snapped wife - dead husband - non-paying case," as I recall. Why he had to go there was out of curiosity, primarily. He just wanted to know if I had decided to take the case or not. Leave it to him to point out statistics he heard while watching 48 hours. None of them were encouraging, and some I preferred not to discuss while eating my lunch.

Everywhere I turned it seemed as though someone was pointing me in the direction of that case. Teddy made it a point to mention solving a case like that could bring in a lot of business. He was always focused on the dollars to be made. The kid constantly pestered me to pursue it as well even though she had no idea what it entailed, and Wally was the one that sent Mrs. Grayson to me to start with, he was the one I really needed to talk to.

The truth was I had never declined to take any case Wally sent my way. I just liked to act as though I kept my options open. Sometimes, I fought internally with myself about the merit of a particular case or the probability of solving it, but in the end I worked it no matter what. It became clear while standing there finishing what was left of my bratwurst that if I was going to find the kid's aunt, and determine what actually happened to Mrs. Grayson's husband, I was going to have to make arrangements for someone to watch Kelsey. I couldn't exactly drag her downtown to the police station with me to talk to cops. I had plenty of work to do to track down her aunt as well. Searching through records and talking to Wally wouldn't have exactly been "Funville" for her, and a trip to the medical examiner's office was out of the question.

When I told Joe what the problem was with working that case he volunteered to hang out with the kid while I did my detective thing. I thought he was in for a fair amount of grief with that offer, but Cheeseburger and the kid could spend all day together, and never tire of one another. Who was I to look a gift horse in the mouth - whatever that means. That was Willard's old saying, and he had plenty of them. I asked if the kid was up for hanging out with them while I got some work done, and she agreed that was a great idea. "Alright," Joe said. "Tomorrow, I'm putting you to work. You know how to sell lemonade?"

"The kid said, "no, but I like to drink it."

"Then you have what it takes to sell it then. You have to love your product. That's the first rule in any business."

It was a win, win as I like to call it. Kelsey got to hang out with Cheeseburger. Cheeseburger got extra hotdog to eat, and pats on the head. Joe had a new draw to his hotdog stand with his newest employee, a forty-two inch tall lemonade vender, and I had the ability to start working the cases I needed to solve without her under my feet.

I placed a call to Wally telling him I needed to speak with him about Mrs. Grayson's case if he wanted me to take it, and I preferred to do it in person. Wally was always up for a visit, life in the records room could get pretty lonely at times. Half the cases he sent my way, I was certain he did it just to bring some excitement into his world. This one brought with it, its' share of challenges. I told him I'd meet him tomorrow afternoon, and I asked him to pull whatever reports or case files he had on Mr. Grayson, also the lead investigator's notes would be helpful as well. Wally sounded eager to help when he said, "I'm on it," just before I hung up the phone.

He like several others I came in contact with on a regular basis fancied themselves as my partner in a way, or so it seemed. If they had any idea how little detective work paid they would have steered clear of me and this business altogether. You might be thinking, come on Pepper. Here you are charging wealthy women thousands of dollars to spy on their husbands, and yet you're always grumbling about money being tight. You have to have a stash of some kind put away for a rainy day. The truth was everyday poured for me in Boston, and I stayed broke.

Where did all the money go? I don't know, I'm no accountant but gathering information worth having always costs something in the end. I can tell you that informants want money, and people in places able to help you have a price tag as well. Between what it took to recover stolen property and conduct person to person interviews along with data searches, locating hard to find witnesses, and traveling to out of the way places, to follow leftover leads found at crime scenes money had a way of disappearing quick. Not to mention, independent lab forensics costs out the wazoo. It was my job though and many times the course of action taken in a case was determined by how much of the green stuff was on hand at the time. So, I guess you could say the fine art of staying in business as a private investigator hinges on your ability to gather information worth having for next to nothing. I had been at it for a while. So, take it for what it's worth. It wasn't all glitz and glamour.

Chapter 34

Breakfast With Kelsey

The next morning, I found myself sprawled out in my chair behind my desk. The sun once again served as my alarm clock as I felt blindly on my desk for my hat, but it wasn't where I placed it before I drifted off to sleep. That's when I heard something moving about next to me. Don't worry, it wasn't a rat this time or some guy holding a gun to my head. It was still startling though when I woke up to find the kid wearing my hat as she shoved a bowl full of cereal at me saying, "here. I made it just the way you like it."

It was cornflakes floating in coca cola. It looked delicious, like something found in the toilet on a bad day. I stared at it a moment as she held it in front of me. It was tan and brown, much like the rat that spent the afternoon in my office a week earlier. Except the rat would have been easier to get rid of quick, a trail of cheese out into the hallway and he'd be someone else's problem to deal with. As for what the kid had stuffed in front of me, it didn't look so appetizing. Okay, it looked disgusting. "Aren't you going to eat it," she asked.

"Yeah, sure," I said as she handed it to me. "Where's the spoon?" I was still half asleep.

"Oh, I knew I forgot something."

She turned to grab the spoon and I sat the tasty looking concoction down on my desk saying, "you know what, let's do something a little different this morning. What do you say to pancakes?"

"I don't know how to make those sorry, but you can teach me."

"No. I don't know how to make them either kid, but I

know some place that does, come on, I'll take you there."

"Okay but first…"

"I know, you gotta go."

"Yeah, and don't time me this time okay."

I looked at my watch just to see what time it really was as I said, "okay but hurry up or we'll miss breakfast."

"I will jeez, I swear."

"Don't swear, it's not ladylike."

"What do you know about being a lady?"

"I've known plenty of them, and they don't swear."

"Do you have a girlfriend?"

"Do you have to go to the bathroom or not?"

"Okay, I'm going."

Once we were finally in the car she had another question for me. "Where are we going?"

"You'll see," I said.

"Are you taking me to Burger King?"

"No, no Burger King."

"I like Burger King."

"Yeah. Well, there's no Burger King around here kid."

"Do they have a slide?"

"No, no slide."

"What about toys?"

"Yeah. I think they do. I don't know."

"This doesn't sound like a very fun place."

"Well it is."

"We'll see."

"Look kid, all I know is they have pancakes. You want to eat something other than old cornflakes, then this is the only place I know of where we can afford to eat that's close by."

"I thought you said you liked that cereal."

"No one likes that cereal, are you kidding me."

"Then why did you buy it?"

"I bought it cause it was cheap."

"That doesn't make any sense."

"Trust me kid, someday it will."

Just about the time I finished saying that, my diner came into view up the street. Kelsey was looking out the window taking in the scenery on the way there. "Here we are," I said, as I pulled into a parking space next to it.

She scrunched up her nose asking, "this is it?"

"Yeah, come on. You'll like it I promise."

"I don't think so."

"Hey, they've got pie here."

That's when she informed me pie was for old people. Well, she was probably right on that, I liked pie and the more time I spent around the kid the older I felt. To prove my point further, I never met an old person that didn't like pie. They never turned down a piece if they were offered. It was their universal indulgence it seemed. Maybe they lived long enough to know you should take advantage of anything in this world that's pleasing and tasty while you are given the chance. That's how I looked at it anyway. It was only logical once someone hit seventy, time became shorter than it once was, and it was time to eat all the pie one could hold.

As we entered My Diner several of the waitresses had to make over Kelsey. To them I was nothing special. They saw me on a regular basis, and I always opted for a seat in Gina's section cause I like her. She had personality and curves that could get any guys attention. Sometimes, she took her sweet time in getting to me but I never complained. That morning was different, she made it over to my table in record time with a pencil in hand ready to jot down our order. "What can I do you for today honey?"

Kelsey found her remark amusing as Gina enquired who I had brought with me. I made the introductions and said, "today we're going for the pancakes."

Gina asked Kelsey if she wanted strawberries on hers along with a whip cream smiley face. I was compelled to ask, "you can do that?"

She fired back, "sweetie, I can do anything."

Immediately, my mind went somewhere else. She leaned over to show the kid a picture on the back of her menu of the happy face pancake breakfast, and I adjusted my head to get a better look for myself. It's important to know what you're buying. I'm prudent like that. Gina turned toward me, and I pulled my eyes away from her cleavage as I said, "I didn't see that. She must have some kind of special menu over there." Gina informed me it was on my menu too, all I had to do is look for it. My reply was, "I'm looking alright," as she flipped to it for me.

She mocked me a little saying, "if a detective can't find it, I don't know who can."

That's when she flashed me a smile and that smile was why I made My Diner, my diner. In all fairness, I had never noticed the happy face pancake breakfast before, because I never looked at the kid's menu, and even when Gina showed it to me there were other things obstructing my view. I asked, "those come with free toppings?"

"That's right, any topping you want?"

"Then I'll have mine the same way I guess, and some orange juice, but I want the blueberry pancakes. Can you do that for me?"

"I think you qualify as being able to eat off the kids menu."

With that, she sashayed away with our menus telling us they'd be right up, and the kid just had to say, "you like her, don't you."

"What makes you say that? She's nice isn't she?"

"You like her."

"Do your picture find puzzle."

The kid seemed to like the place. They didn't have toys, but they were equipped with plenty of crayons. That evidently goes a long way with seven year olds. As far as the food went, it beat coca cola cornflakes hands down any day of the week, and eating a plate of short stack pancakes dissecting the smiley face piece by piece was more enjoyable than one might think. Maybe it had something to do with the company I was in, and the extra attention I received from the other waitresses. The kid evidently was good for my image in their eyes.

When we finished our plates, Kelsey had to try out their milkshakes. Gina took that opportunity to offer me a piece of free pie. You know what I told you about where I stood when it came to pie. I wasn't turning that down, not coming from Gina. She had never offered me free pie before, no matter how much I flirted with her. Yes, it was shaping out to be a good morning indeed. Seeing the time, I realized I was cutting it close. Wally was expecting me, and Joe and Cheeseburger were anticipating Kelsey's arrival soon.

Gina made a final trip by our table asking if there was anything else she could get me. My response was, "maybe next time." I laid the tip on the table telling her I'd definitely be back, and Kelsey felt the need to inform her I liked her. The kid liked putting me on the spot, but Gina confessed, "well, I like Pepper too."

She then said something about how cute the kid was. I didn't really pay much attention to that part. I was still clinging to the fact she was into me, but I played it cool saying, "kids, you never know what they're going to say, do you." We exited the restaurant and climbed in the car. It was time to go to work.

Chapter 35

Taking Care Of Business

A quick trip back to my office, a potty visit for the kid, and a stop by Teddy's shine chair to say hey, and it was time to drop Kelsey off with Joe, and meet with Wally before contacting Mrs. Grayson. The ironic thing was once Teddy found out the kid was hanging out with Joe and Cheeseburger for the day, he began to try and convince me the kid should hang out there with him, indoors, out of the elements, right close to the restrooms. "Why she can even have the extra chair. It's not like I can shine two pairs of shoes at once." That was his sales pitch. Teddy could shine two pairs at once, I had seen him do it, but he wanted her to keep him company between customers.

The kid kept me busier than a soccer mom with triplets. At least I didn't have to take her to ballet class, thank God. Although, those ballerina instructors probably have a damn good set of legs on them I imagine. I should've probably looked into that for the kid's sake just in case it took longer to find her aunt than I hoped. I said, "let me check with Joe and see what her schedule looks like for the rest of the week. I'm sure we can fit you in somewhere."

It seemed I was going to have no shortage of willing kid watchers in my absence. Joe and Cheeseburger were ready for Kelsey as soon as we arrived. With a brief explanation of why we were running late, Joe made out as if his hotdog stand couldn't be run without her. The lemonade was mixed and ready to pour. Joe let me sample some, and then he hit me up for a dollar as he told Kelsey to tell all the customers she made it herself, he figured he could sell more that way. I set out to meet Wally telling Kelsey, "see you later kid."

She paid me little attention though as Joe promptly placed a hat on her head handing her a set of tongs. He then informed her, "I'm putting you in charge of toppings kid. That's an important part of the business." Joe was confident saying, "we're going to sell a lot of hotdogs today. I can feel it." I must admit the kid was kind of cute, and Joe was right, she'd probably increase his sales by twenty percent simply by being herself, asking people if they wanted to add some peppers or pickle relish. I left her in his care knowing she'd be fine as Joe taught her the ins and outs of how to up-sale folks. "You never want to miss an opportunity," was the last instruction I heard Joe hand her as I walked out of earshot.

On my way to meet Wally, I stopped off at Walgreens to take care of some business. Lester, the guy in the photo lab always looked forward to developing my prints. In fact, he personally processed each roll of film I left in his care, cause frankly, sometimes the pictures I took could be rather risqué in nature.

If he was training someone on the equipment, or his assistant tried to take care of me, he always intervened. He would whisper every time he spoke to me whenever another customer would happen to pass by us as if we were planning something covert. The need he felt to keep things secretive was both humorous and reassuring.

He liked to use signals to communicate half the time to avoid drawing other people's attention. A slight nod of the head or a wink was quite typical, but either way Lester's feeling of importance increased tenfold when he saw me walk through the door with that camera in my hand. That's why I used him for all my processing, I suppose. That, and I had a deal with Walgreens where I got my film free. All I had to do was pay Lester to develop it for me. You can't find a deal better than that anywhere, or I would've uncovered it, me being the sleuth that I am. So, maybe it wasn't all about our working relationship. Anyway, Lester used terminology like, "I'll make sure to keep this on the down-low cause I know what the deal-e-o is.

I'd just try not to laugh when I said, "I'd appreciate that."

He was a bit of a dramatic hipster in a way. He was born with a vintage name decades after his time, I'd say, but I found him competent and incredibly amusing at times. He knew what I did for a living, and he thought it was pretty cool. He probably figured my life was filled with high-profile cases, dead bodies, sorted affairs, lots of loose women and guns. Where he dreamed all that up I have no idea. What can I say, it didn't take much to impress a guy like Lester. He spent eight hours of his life every day of the week in a ten by twelve corner of a retail store developing photographs of other people's lives, while his waited on hold.

Before handing him the camera I said, "this one's important." That gave him that twinkle in his eye, the one that shouted - that's why I took this job in the first place. Screw the nine-fifty an hour.

In true spy fashion, I slid him the camera. After taking the handoff, he pulled out the film bagging it, and tagging it as he replied, "I got you. Mission critical, I'll put a rush on it. It'll be ready when you are." That was Lester for you. With a nod of the head I was almost out of there. Pausing long enough to grab a snickers bar on my way out of the store I picked up the Sports Illustrated Swimsuit Calendar.

It was on the closeout rack, and I'm a bargain shopper as you know. I'll say this, it was eye-catching, and a whole lot more, but it wasn't for me. If I was meeting Wally, I might need a bargaining chip just in case I asked him to do something he shouldn't that he thought could get him fired. What better gift could you get a forty-five year old guy without a girlfriend who kept his nose buried in file folders?

Photographs of swimsuit models wearing next to nothing were something his mother wouldn't approve of, but he could keep it at his office, and gain the admiration of some of the officers that ventured down to the records room on occasion. So, actually I was Wally's best friend as you can see, always doing my part to look out for him any way I ccould.

Still, he always tended to worry about me getting him into trouble whenever I prodded him to cross one of the bureaucratic lines that surrounded him. Sometimes, my persistent nature came in the form of a pep-talk when you got down to it. That's what it usually took to make Wally feel invincible enough to let me take a look at a file that wasn't part of the public record, but what I found worked best was complete and total distraction.

Truth was they couldn't fire Wally no matter what he did. He was a government employee with tenure, and without him they'd never locate a file in the records room. He had job security woven into his unique filing system, and he didn't even realize it. It often took me to remind him of that, and something like a swimsuit calendar was just what the place needed.

Chapter 36

A Good Talk With Wally

I pulled into the parking lot across from the police station as my phone rang. It was Mrs. Burke. She wanted a status update on her husband's case including his present whereabouts. I jockeyed for a spot as she carried the conversation. She had a few choice words to say about the woman she suspected him of having an affair with, and she didn't utter them lightly. I had to put her on speakerphone. She practically left me hearing impaired, but I told her it would be best to meet in person at that point.

On the backend of a case like hers getting paid was my top priority, but she needed the pictures which I was having developed as we spoke. I was fairly certain she would've gladly paid top dollar for them, but we had already agreed to two thousand. I explained I was still working her case, but I felt certain it would be closed soon. As she pressed me for details I told her, "right now, I'm outside the courthouse, and I have to meet someone, but let's arrange to meet back at my office say around five if that's good for you." She agreed and I headed inside to see my favorite file clerk.

When I walked into the police station, I was ignored by those that knew me as well as those that didn't. I didn't need directions though. I knew where I could find Wally hard at work. Entering the records room, I found him munching on Fritos, sipping a diet Coke as he read over one of the countless case files. "Find anything interesting in there," I asked as I walked over to his desk concealing the swimsuit edition under my arm.

At first, Wally seemed glad to see me. He greeted me with, "hey, Pepper." Then he added, "you're here about that lady's husband. I just gave your name to her the other day. She didn't waste any time getting a hold of you. Did she?"

I answered him saying, "no, I guess not, but that's why I'm here, that and this." I handed Wally the calendar. His eyes widened, they appeared magnified behind the lenses in his glasses.

He leaned forward putting down the folder he held in his hand asking, "what's that?"

"Oh, just a little something to help you keep up with the days of the week." Pointing to the picture of one of the half-naked swimsuit models I added, "if you don't know what that is it's probably high-time you found out."

He took a closer look at the calendar uttering the word, "whoa."

"Whoa is right my friend." I looked around the place as I said, "thought you could use it to bring a little life into this room."

Immediately, he looked up at me asking, "what do you want?"

"Who says I want anything? I just came by to give you that and talk to you about the case you sent my way. How do you happen to know Mrs. Grayson by the way."

"Oh," I don't really know her that well. She had just made several requests to have us send a copy of the police report to her insurance company. I felt really sorry for her when she told me how the insurance company was treating her. So, I turned her onto you."

"Well, I appreciate that. Mind if I look at that report?"

Wally stared at the calendar as I asked the question. He muttered, "sure, help yourself." His attention was focused on Miss February's two piece at that moment, and who could really blame him, she wore it well.

"I'm also going to need a copy of the death certificate,

and the autopsy reports, but you can get those for me right."

"Yeah, whatever you need."

Wally set the calendar down on his desk long enough to look up the records for me on his computer. Still, his eyes diverted to it occasionally as he paused from typing, but he managed to direct me to the correct file. I asked if he could print off the coroner's report so we could get a better look at it, and he obliged that request as well. So far, the Sports Illustrated Calendar was working its' magic for me. Wally just drew the line at me leaving the records room taking that information with me, but I usually managed to get my way in the end.

What the medical examiner's report said was a bit beyond my intellectual reach. Don't laugh, it was full of big words that made little sense to a fella like me. Half of it I couldn't begin to pronounce. Wally could, but he knew very little medical terminology himself. Reading over it he offered, "I think lividity in this case has something to do with blood pooling." He looked at me with the unsure expression planted on his mug.

I pointed to part of his summary. "Do you know what the hell he's talking about here," I questioned." That part of the report read, "subject shows signs of congelatio causing severe ecchymosis below the cervicis. Capillary condition remained persistent throughout the mid and lower torso, and found most prevalent in the lower extremities. Minimal body burns were also found on the decedent not inconsistent with electrocution. Trace amounts of chemicals including a high concentration of ethyl alcohol and benzyl ammonium chloride along with narcotics, primarily cocaine were present in the nasal cavities, but not in the bloodstream. Cranial contusion bordering on acute hematoma was also noted but not the cause of death, probably sustained prior to electric shock or during."

Wally looked up some of the terms saying, "that just means he hit his head on something at some point, probably when he fell in the hot tub." Even I knew that.

Things were simple in Wally's world. He had case files piled high holding explicit information concerning unfortunate events and people that caused them. Many of them deliberately hurt others, and thought nothing of it. Still, he managed not to see what I couldn't help but lean toward, and that was people will kill one another given means and proper motive. Especially, if they feel they can get away with it. What better place to do it other than a hot tub. The cleaning chemicals discovered in Mr. Grayson's nasal passages could be occupational hazard or point to a cover up. Either way, I was fairly certain the cocaine found there had nothing to do with his job.

In my line of work accidental deaths seldom crossed my desk, but there were a few. They were more complex than most I assure you, but maybe just enough to keep me from losing faith in the entire human race. That was often the only comfort they provided me with though.

Wally admired his gift noting, "this calendar is for this year."

"Yeah, so what."

"Well this year is almost over," he complained.

"Well, I can take it back if you don't won't it, but these things are hard to come by."

"Yeah, I hear they're collector's items."

"Well, I'd collect them if I were you. You never know what the things might be worth someday."

"Yeah, I just don't have anywhere to put it."

I tried to help the guy out, do the thinking for him. "Why not stick it over there?" I pointed to an empty spot on the side of his filing cabinet next to his desk. Pulling a piece of scotch tape off the large roll sitting directly in front of him I said, "try this. You don't mind if I take what you printed off for me do you?"

He was almost in a fog. "No," he replied. He hesitated a little as he spoke mentioning, "I don't think I can put this up where people can see it."

"Why not?"

"Well, we have several female officers on the force now, and sometimes Bridget brings folders down here from upstairs. I mean what would they think seeing this hanging there?"

Wally had a thing for Bridget ever since she first walked into his life carrying a stack of police reports. You'd have thought he'd made it to second base when he finally managed to convince her to join him for lunch every other Thursday in the records room. He did it under the guise of it being a departmental meeting.

I simply pointed out, "they'd probably think you're into women and sports. How bad could that be for your image?" Wally snatched the tape out of my hand, and he plastered the calendar to the side of his filing cabinet feeling, a bit more manly than he did when I first entered the room. I thanked him for his help, and promised to get to the bottom of Mrs. Grayson's case for him. Maybe that didn't come out right, but you know what I'm trying to say. I complimented his decorating taste as I headed for the door with a copy of the police findings, and the coroner's report in hand. Wally continued admiring his gift as he thanked me for it. He didn't even question when I was going to return the file folder to him, God I love women in bikinis. Did I happen to mention Wally was the man?

Chapter 37

A Trip To The Morgue

With me being the gifted intellectual I am, based on my extensive experience researching complex medical matters, not to mention my numerous scholastic achievements which left me hindered in pronouncing my own over the counter medications, it was quite evident to me at that point, I needed serious assistance. Luckily, for me I had someone to turn to in times like that, and there was always one person I knew I could count on to shoot it to me straight in layman's terms. That person was Craig Fetch, of course, and he was always more than happy to help. He worked part time in the hospital morgue, and he was a fulltime student at the university. The other thing I can tell you about Fetch is he knew his shit. There was no two ways about it, and occasionally he helped me solve cases simply by filling in a few holes for me. Quite frankly, he loved investigative work, and he jumped at the chance to give me a hand whenever I needed it.

I entered the hospital and took the elevator down to the place where they kept the unlucky patients. I hated hospitals, I'll admit it, but flirting with nurses happened to be my specialty. Only thing was there was no time for that. I had to pick up the pictures I'd dropped off with Lester, and get back before Joe closed up shop, and called it a day. On top of that, whenever I needed to stop by the morgue, I usually had to keep a low profile. That's a little more difficult than one might think, but borrowing a check-in clipboard on my way in along with a lab coat from the laundry was usually my ticket to make it down to Fetch's part of the building with a little help, no questions asked and a badge swipe from one of the orderlies.

Fetch found himself completely caught off guard seeing me enter the freezer unannounced. I was fortunate to find him there though, and I told him that pretty much as he asked, "Pepper. What in the hell are you doing down here?"

Okay, so maybe he wasn't totally stoked to see me, but he was a friend, right. I reminded him of that. Then I gave him some spiel about can't a guy drop by and say hey whenever he happens to be in the area. He gave me the once over from the other side of the room, admiring my choice in attire he made note of the clipboard and lab coat. "You're not supposed to be down here."

"I know that, I'm a doctor for Pete's sake. I just have a little favor I need to ask of you." Our discussions usually always started off like that for some reason.

"The answer is, no."

"That's being closed minded. We talked about that, remember."

He reiterated the word "no" as if it had some important meaning. "But you haven't even heard the request, yet."

"Look, I'm not swapping any toe-tags for you, and I'm not performing an unauthorized corpse analysis. You almost got me in deep trouble for that."

He kind of looked toward the door as he spoke making sure no one heard what he was saying. The guy was a little paranoid at times. What can I say? He and Wally would have made quite a pair, but with Fetch, I could usually guilt him into just about anything, not that I'm proud of that, but it worked. You have to appreciate a man with a conscience, they're hard to find this day and age.

"Look, I'm not here to ask you to do anything I wouldn't do, okay."

The miffed expression on his face said almost as much as his words did.

"Is that supposed to make me feel any better," he questioned with a great deal of sarcasm embedded in his voice.

"Hey, how was I to know the defense attorney was going to question what I deemed expert testimony? Besides, I managed to keep you from having to take the stand in that case. Didn't I?"

He, of course, had to agree with me as I pointed out I was always looking out for him. Then I played the guilt card cause it was as good a time as any. "You know I just thought you'd want to help this widow woman I'm working a case for. I mean she's got no money to pay me, and the insurance company is trying to screw her, but I figured you'd want to help me help her by just reading over this report and explaining some things to me."

He stood there looking at me holding what appeared to be an x-ray in his left hand. "I guess I may have been wrong for once, maybe you don't care about her at all or what happened to her husband. Mr. Grayson is his name, just in the off chance you were wondering."

Like clockwork the x-ray Fetch was holding landed on the table in front of where he was standing. With a heavy breath and a sigh of relief he said, "well, why didn't you just say so in the first place? Let me see what you have there."

He took a minute to peruse the coroner's report as I looked back at the police investigator's statements. "Hmmm." He said that three times as he read the report a second time. "That's odd," he admitted.

"Care to share," I asked.

Says here the subject showed signs of ruptured capillaries

in various parts of the body, mainly concentrated in the lower extremities. I've heard of that being seen when electric shock is the cause of death, but it's usually confined to a specific region."

"You're talking point of contact."

"Yeah, basically and within eight to twelve inches thereof. The surface of the skin can show a burn based on conditions, but I've never seen anything like that. I guess anything is possible. It also says Mr. Grayson suffered a blow to the head. However, that was determined to not be the cause of death. Where was he found?"

"In his hot tub. Police found him floating with his stereo submerged. What would cause capillary ruptures to occur inside the water like that?"

"Good question, the temperature of the water would have to be extremely hot to cause the redness shown on the skin here, but the burned areas would be consistent with contact with the water."

"So, it's not normal."

I pointed to a photograph taken by police. Mr. Grayson wasn't holding his best pose in it at the time, and the shot itself was rather revealing. Grayson's back and buttocks appeared immune to the heat from the hot tub. Parts of his legs and arms also showed no signs of discoloration. I'm no medic, but I wished to know the answer to that based on Fetch's remarks.

"Well, that's weird," he admitted. "Maybe it had to do with the position the body was in at some point."

"Perhaps he was sitting when the stereo entered the tub."

"Well, like I said, that appears to be pretty extensive. The places where the skin shows discoloration just seem off. I guess if they found him in the water it would be difficult to determine the placement of the body when Mr. Grayson actually suffered the shock, but those types of ruptures on that scale often coincide with what's commonly known as frostbite. How in the hell do you manage to get frostbit in a hot tub?"

"That's the hundred thousand dollar question, isn't it." There was a lot going on in that report. "What's the time of death listed as?"

"9:20 a.m. Friday morning. Hey, this guy must have really liked to party."

Fetch was making reference to the mention of cocaine being present in the coroner's report.

"Well, his wife was out of town."

"That explains it."

I looked at him, appreciating his cynicism, then I asked, "do you know of anyone taking a dip in their hot tub at that hour?"

"Somebody not into taking showers, I guess." Fetch could see I wasn't buying that one. That's when he offered, "well, that's a little odd I guess, but I don't own a hot tub."

"Me either. Is there any way that time of death could be incorrect?"

"Temperature of the water could throw it off some, sure. Actually, based on that it really depends on the water temperature at the time when they found him. Are you looking at an accident or a suicide cause I could think of a better way to go than that."

"I bet, but we might not be looking at either one."

"How are you going to go about proving that?"

"A little digging and maybe a little more help from you."

I looked in the direction of one of the empty cooler compartments. Immediately, a thought came to mind, and Fetch noticed. "You're not digging up the body are you?" Right away he began saying, "oh, no. You're not bringing him here. Hospital guidelines strictly prohibit any dead bodies being brought in this room that haven't been admitted to the hospital for treatment prior to death."

"I know the rules, don't get all squeamish on me now. I just had an idea hit me that's all."

"I know, that's what concerns me. Now, you've got to get the hell out of here."

"Actually, I do, but I want you to determine how far that time of death could have been off for me." That left Fetch with something to think about. "Alright," he said, "but next time call before you drop by, and stop stealing uniforms."

I tugged at the lapel of the lab coat saying, "this is just a loaner," and with that I was out the door.

Chapter 38

A Case With Glitches

I was cutting it close to my appointed meeting time with Mrs. Burke. When I arrived to pick up the photos Lester had promised would be ready when I was, I had a surprise waiting on me. Lester was having difficulty printing the pictures. His machine was on the fritz. So, the photos weren't ready and Lester's feet were the only part of him showing, extending out from underneath the drying conveyer when I called his name looking for him behind the counter. "I'm down here," he said with frustration in his voice.

Working intently with a screwdriver and his hands, he uttered an expletive pinching his finger in one of the gear wheels. "I need those pictures bad," I said. "But I don't think I'm willing to do that for them." It was a vain attempt to add humor to the situation. "Are you okay under there?" He forced me to ask as he squirmed some groaning while lying there on the floor. Lester's back wasn't the best in the world, and now I knew the reason for it.
"I'd be better if I could get this machine up and running."
"Well, that would make two of us, I'm sure."

Lester was the kind of guy that never gave up on something. I guess you could say he'd be a good guy to have around when all seemed hopeless, but even he was nearing the end of his rope with this machine malfunction. He pulled himself out from under the conveyer, straining a little to stand. It was clear he had been at it for a while. According to him the damn thing went down almost right after I left. The other thing about Lester I forgot to mention is, he didn't have the best of luck. Okay quite frankly, his luck sucked and that's putting it mildly, but now it was causing me grief. Lester confessed, "I've done all I know to do, Pepper. I might have to call a professional in on this one."

I offered my expert opinion at that point. "Well what the hell is wrong with it? It looks okay to me, just put the cover back on it."

"Something's wrong with one of the gears inside the machine. I can't get it to budge at all."

"So, bypass it if you have to. That's what I'd do."

"Well, this isn't like heart surgery, it doesn't actually work like that."

"Sure it would, all you'd have to do is take them out of there and feed them in that thing over there."

Lester hated to break it to me, but my pictures weren't going to be ready anytime soon. He told me he'd call me as soon as he had them, but not to expect to hear from him before tomorrow afternoon. I didn't want to postpone my meeting with Mrs. Burke. It was time to get paid, and I loved that part of this business more than anything else. Mrs. Burke was the type of woman that was used to having things her way. She wouldn't understand delaying our meeting, but what choice did I have.

I left out of there wishing Lester luck. I then had to reschedule with Mrs. Burke, and pick the kid up. We also had to make a trip to the grocery store. It was looking like the kid was going to be in my care a little longer than I first anticipated upon meeting her.

Mrs. Burke wasn't pleased, but I managed to explain it was going to take some time to get what she wanted. You never confirm with a client their suspicions were correct before getting paid. That was a bad way of doing business, and a sure way to screw yourself out of money. What I needed to hand her in exchange for the remaining fifteen hundred was proof her husband was doing his secretary, and Lester had that proof stuck inside his photo developer. He made no mention of damage being sustained to the negatives. So, I naturally assumed I'd have them within a day or two.

Chapter 39

A Long Night With Kelsey

Joe had nothing but praise for the kid when I finally arrived to take her off his hands, and Kelsey had plenty to tell me about her day. Joe had already made out a tentative work schedule for the kid, and wasted no time in clearing it with me. He wanted her back at the usual time first thing Monday, and Kelsey seemed excited about it. It was clear she liked hanging out with Joe and his dog. She was less excited about where we were headed when I told her we had errands to run, but full of questions as usual.

"Where to now?"

"We're going to the store."

"It's dark."

"I know. That's the best time to go shop, no one's there at night."

"So, that's cause it's dark."

"Look, there's no one there. That means you get in, and out with no hassles. No waiting in line on someone fiddle-farting around trying to get their reward bucks."

Kelsey laughed a little. "What's funny now?"

"You said fiddle-farting."

"I did. Sorry kid, forget I ever said that. It doesn't mean what you think I assure you."

Note to self - watch what I say around the seven year old, she liked repeating that phrase too. She did it until I told her to stop. Then she asked, "so, what are we shopping for?"

"We're going grocery shopping kid."

"Oh cool, I'll get the buggy."

"We don't need a cart kid. We're only grabbing bread and

milk nothing else."

"I thought you didn't like milk."

"I don't, but you do, and you need something to eat."

"Can we please get a buggy, I like to ride in it. Hey, you can push me."

"This isn't six flags kid, it's a store."

"But no one's here like you said. Besides, we might find something else we want."

"Like what?"

"I don't know ice cream, chocolate cake, or maybe some cookies, cookies are good."

"I'll tell you what, you can ride in the cart, but we stick to the list. You got it?"

"Where's the list?" She climbed in the cart, and I raised my hand tapping my finger next to the side of my head as I spoke, "it's all up here kid."

She looked at me and she shook her head saying, "boy are we in trouble."

I began to push her trying not to laugh at her cutting remark which was actually quite humorous. I said, "oh yeah, hang on kid." I'm telling you she really liked riding in that cart.

As we made a hairpin turn onto isle three she extended her arms out to each side leaning forward toward the front of the grocery buggy as she yelled, "faster Pepper, faster!" The kid reminded me of Leonardo DiCaprio hanging off the bow of that sinking ship in the movie *Titanic*. Thirty minutes later we arrived at the register with the cart half full of things Kelsey had to have. She even talked me into buying a box of the good cereal for a change. She swore up and down it tastes better. All I was looking at was the price, but she made a convincing sales pitch when she said, "I'll eat it if you don't like it, and I won't complain about it at all." Yeah that was the closer for me.

Admittedly, I never cared for going to the store, it was a pain in the ass most of the time, and a chore like everything else in my adult life, but shopping for food with the kid was anything other than boring. Hell, I'd almost say it was fun. There you have it. Are you happy now? Anyway, she must have had a good time because she asked when we could come back again. I opened the door to the Fairlane, and loaded two bags into the backseat as I told her, "we'll see kid." This time she took that answer for what it was worth. I guess we were making progress.

That night I spent the better part of my time searching for known addresses Rhea Fallon once lived at, and I compiled a small list of people that might have some clue to her whereabouts, starting with her previous employer from six years back. It was an accounting firm known to many as Humphrey and Doyle. I didn't know how long she worked there, or even what she did for them, but that was the first place I planned to visit as soon as they opened Monday morning. In the meantime, I had former landlords and neighbors to try and track down to interview, and even though the chances were slim that they could lead me to her, I had to follow up with them. It was standard detective protocol and sometimes you managed to get lucky.

Questions lingered in my mind about what caused the skin irritation which covered much of Mr. Grayson's lower body. Fetch and I were both puzzled by the irregular patterns and burn regions. Those questions had to wait to be answered though, since I intentionally refrained from opening the reports until the kid went to sleep before investing any further effort into figuring out what happened to Mr. Grayson.

I didn't want her to know any more than she already did,

and I was fairly certain she had no business seeing what I did in the police photos. I didn't what her to remember Mr. Grayson that way. It was bad enough she constantly referred to him as the dead guy. Some images you just never get rid of, and I was hoping she would forget about him entirely. Out of sight, out of mind, I guess you could say. It's not likely I know, but one can hope.

Trying to get the kid to turn in though was slightly more challenging than I anticipated. I told her to lay down and close her eyes, and she informed me that wasn't working. "Try counting sheep," I said, but that only spurned her to question why. I didn't really have a good answer for that. It had never made any sense to me either. So, I attempted to bore her to sleep telling about one of my less eventful days spent behind this desk, but she didn't want to hear it. Instead she made a request.

"Will you read me a bedtime story?"

"What kind of story?"

"A bedtime story, you know, like Snow White and Cinderella. I like Sleeping Beauty too, but my favorite is Horton."

"Never heard of him. Who's Horton?"

"No, it's Horton Hears A Who."

"He hears a what?"

"Not a what, a who. Don't you know anything?"

"Evidently, this Horton guy and I haven't met."

"He's not a guy, he's an elephant silly."

"Oh. Well, that explains it."

"Explains what?"

"I don't know any elephants. Go to sleep kid."

"Come on, you have to know at least one story."

"The only bedtime story I know has three bears in it."

"I don't like that one."

"Good that saves me from having to tell it to you."

"Are you sure you don't know any others."

"Yeah, I know one more."

"Well what is it?"

"Don't worry, you won't like it."

"How do you know I won't like it?"

"Cause you're a woman of discerning tastes."

"What's that mean?"

"That means you're picky kid."

"No, I'm not."

"I think you are."

"I'm just a kid tell it to me anyway. What's it about?"

"Three little pigs."

"Do you know any that don't start with the number three?"

"Nope. Told you, you wouldn't like it."

"Tell it to me anyway."

"But you won't like it."

"Maybe it will be better if you tell it instead of my grandma. I bet you could do a great wolf voice."

"I'm not doing it."

"You want me to go to sleep, don't you?"

"Three little pigs it is then. There once were these three little pigs you see, and they all needed a place to live, but they couldn't get along with one another so they needed separate places."

"Why didn't they get along?"

"They were brothers, brothers never get along."

"What were their names?"

"What does it matter what their names are?"

"Well, everyone has to have a name. Don't they?"

"These are pigs."

"I can think of some names for them."

"No you can't this is my story. Their names were Martin, Melvin and Mitchell."

"Maybe their names should start with a 'P' since they are pigs."

"Okay, I get what you're saying, Martin Pig doesn't sound good. Scratch those names, they were Patrick, Peter and Preston."

"That's better."

"Okay be quiet and let me tell the story now. So. Like I was saying, Patrick set out to get him some straw to build him a house…"

"And that big old bad wolf gave it his all and he huffed and he puffed, but he couldn't blow that house down no matter how hard he tried, soon he said, "man I give up," and the three little pigs, you know Patrick, Peter and Preston got some more bricks, and added on two additional wings to Preston's house, and when they were done it was like a fortress."

"What's a fortress?"

"It's like a castle."

"Oh, I like castles."

"Yeah. Well, so did these three little pigs, cause the mighty wolf could never blow that house down to have him some bacon, and they lived happily ever after except for the occasional domestic dispute."

"What's that?"

"It's an argument kid."

"Then why didn't you just say that?"

"Well I'm saying it now."

"Okay. Tell me the one about the three bears."

"Close your eyes first." She shut them tight, and I told the story.

Chapter 40

Working A Case In The Dark

It was nearly the next day by the time I got around to opening the folder Wally had given me concerning Mr. Grayson. As midnight approached, I waded through the police report a second time making note of anything else that stood out to me. No blood, no fibers, and virtually no fingerprints were found at the scene other than those belonging to Mr. and Mrs. Grayson.

The scene itself seemed sterile, wiped down if you will. It was easy to do in a hot tub. Most of the evidence worth having could easily be washed away with minimal effort if foul play was involved. I wasn't ruling anything out at this point suicide, accident and murder were still all on the table. Start looking at something only one-sided, and you screw everything up. That's obviously how Delores Grayson wanted me to see it, but she had good reason for that. Andrew Grayson, on the other hand, left this world the same way he came into it, in his birthday suit. Few guys would choose to be discovered uncovered, but it made perfect sense in the case of accident or murder.

The probing investigation took just over two months from the time Mrs. Grayson came home from a personal trip to visit her sister in Charlotte. That's when she found her hubby backside up in their Jacuzzi, talk about your unforgettable welcome home moments. That was one of them, I'm sure. Based on the report from the coroner, and the variables present at the scene, after conferring with Fetch, it was apparent time of death wasn't exact in this case. There was no way it possibly could be.

The lead investigator was Detective Langford. I knew I could probably get some additional information out of him that wasn't listed in the official records. I just had to keep him from finding out I already saw his report. To gain his cooperation, my best angle was to lead him to believe I might be working on behalf of an insurance company which carried a policy with Mr. Grayson's name on it. Of course, if he asked, I'd tell him who had requested my assistance, there would be no getting around that, but what I wished to know couldn't be seen on those pages he filed closing out the case.

I opted for meeting Mrs. Grayson first to explain how I planned to go about conducting the investigation. That would also be an excellent opportunity for me to get her to sign-off on some things to legally pull needed information on her husband. There were obviously other ways to come by that information without her approval, but I saw no reason for it to come to that. If she couldn't give the authorization, then I couldn't work the case, and that's how I planned to put it to her. Why should she have cared? I was willing the do everything she had asked without anything upfront.

I made a few more notes before calling it a night, and that was about one in the morning when I finally closed my notepad. Saturday was already there, and it was shaping out to be a busy one. It was fortunate for me Teddy had agreed to keep an eye on Kelsey for me. He and Joe were virtually rivals when it came to spending time with her now. Joe had her every other day during the week, and Teddy had her Tuesdays and Thursdays. It worked out good for me, the kid too, I guess. As for yours truly, I didn't have to count any sheep myself, not that evening. I just sat back in my chair watching over my special delivery, and that's where I found myself when the sun appeared six hours later. My neck had a crick in it that stayed with me all morning. Old age, and not so easy chairs, just don't go that good together, that's what I learned from that experience. All I can say is, God I missed that sofa.

Chapter 41

Case Setbacks

It was approximately 10:12 Saturday morning when I had left Kelsey in Teddy's capable care with strict instructions for her not to play him in checkers for money. To make my point I said, "I know my pockets look deep, but they're not that deep, kid." Teddy laughed a little. They both found it humorous. That's when I turned to him saying, "and as for you, don't go hustling the kid." She had no idea what that word meant.

Teddy fired back with, "hey, you go on and take care of business, we've got this under control. Don't we?" Kelsey seemed in agreement with Teddy on that note. I just hope the kid listened to me.

I was heading west on Tremont struggling to put my hands on the piece of paper I had stuffed somewhere in my coat. It had several addresses written on it, and I was on my way to check out a former residence Rhea stayed at which wasn't too far from Mrs. Grayson's place. That's when I got the call from Lester, the film I had given him was wasted, chewed up was the way he described it over the phone.

Suddenly, Mrs. Burke's piece-of-cake case was made more difficult. I still had the recording of Mr. Burke, and his secretary doing the deed inside her apartment, but it was worthless without pictures to substantiate it, the money shot remember. That's what she wanted. That meant more time spent doing surveillance for the same money, and possibly putting Mrs. Burke off even longer, topping things off, I really needed the fifteen hundred.

I couldn't get mad at Lester. It wasn't his fault the machine ate the film. If anyone would go the extra mile for me it was him. He apologized numerous times, but I told him I understood. The bright side of it was the photo developer was back in operation, and Lester promised more free film. I could always use plenty of that with the kind of jobs I took.

Not surprisingly, my luck didn't turn out to be any better once I reached Rhea's former residence. The apartment manager had changed twice since she had moved, and no one there in the leasing office seemed to remember her. I asked for the name of the previous manager, and the woman in charge started to give me the runaround. She was dismissive as she spoke claiming they couldn't help me, something about their policies regarding personal information and their inability to put their hands on it.

That forced me to play hardball. So, I pulled a fast one claiming to be a federal investigator working undercover conducting a search for a missing person. Say that firm enough, and fast enough, and you can make people's heads swim. Many times it will get you exactly what you want. She asked to see the badge, and I explained, "undercover agents don't carry credentials cause that can get us killed. Now, I've already told you too much, but I'd appreciate some cooperation cause I really don't want to have to charge you with impeding an investigation. Give me the name of the previous manger or point me to a long time neighbor that might have known her."

Her eyes grew wide and her face went flush as she reached for her chest. How was I supposed to know the woman had a previous heart condition? It wasn't like it was tattooed on her forehead or anything. She looked as though she was about to faint, and I rethought my approach at that very moment. I reached out to catch her helping her into a nearby chair as she stammered saying, "I think I need my heart pills." Sitting there, she winced gritting her teeth in what looked like utter anguish. Another leasing agent went straight to her desk retrieving a small bottle of medicine, and I grabbed her a paper cup filling it full of water.

I guess I went a little too hard on the lady. She looked physically fit enough, but lesson learned. No more throwing the book at an at-risk heart patient unless it was absolutely called for. All I can tell you is she was still breathing without assistance when I left the place, and after the pain in her arm and chest subsided it was time for me to thank them for what little help they had given, and get the hell out before they found out my real name. Let's face it, missing persons cases can be pretty damn dangerous.

Chapter 42

Inspecting the Grayson Place

I promptly arrived to meet Mrs. Grayson ahead of schedule. It gave me a chance to look the place over a little. That was beneficial. The home seemed in need of care, but nothing that screamed it was on the brink of being foreclosed. Although, the picture she had painted for me when we first spoke in my office made it appear she was in dire financial straits.

When she met me at the door, she seemed relieved I was willing to work for nothing basically, but she kept promising to pay me at some point in the future once she could get the money out of the insurance company. I didn't really want to hear it. I had been screwed a time or two before, and I knew what it sounded like early on. I was there strictly out of a sense of duty. If money came from doing what I felt was right, I'd be surprised, but it would be welcomed. However, I wasn't betting on that.

Entering the home, I took a quick look around as I asked her to give me the details of what police found, not sharing with her I'd already reviewed the file. I couldn't help but notice Mrs. Grayson still possessed some nice belongings. She told me briefly about where her husband's body was discovered, and that she called police herself upon finding him right after she had gotten home. I asked her to show me the hot tub, and she led me to another part of the house as I handed her the usual rundown. "Did you notice anything unusual when you returned from your trip, something missing, moved out of place or left open or maybe unlocked?"

She paused only for a second giving it thought. Then she quickly said, "no. Why?"

"Well those are good indicators someone else may have been in the home that normally wasn't here. How often did your husband make use of the Jacuzzi?"

"Maybe a couple times a month," she replied.

"Any particular times he preferred to use it?"

"Sometime in the morning if his back was hurting him, but usually on weekends late in the afternoon, I suppose."

She had all the time slots covered with that answer, so it didn't offer much help. "And did he prefer to wear swim trunks or was he an all-natural kind of guy?"

She hesitated to answer that one. "Well what does that matter," she questioned.

"Maybe I should rephrase the question. Was he wearing anything when you discovered his body?"

Yes, no questions were hard to dodge cause there was only one right answer, and Mrs. Grayson went with, "no."

"Did you find that to be unusual?"

She paused before answering that one saying, "not really."

I had asked the next question many times during my investigative career in various cases, it was a constant in my line of work. Getting a straight answer to it was difficult, people liked to brush it off with the word "okay" if they could get away with it, but I always pressed a little further. Like Willard used to say, "people lie because the truth usually sucks, but pinch them long enough, and hard enough, and they'll squeal telling you a tale worth hearing." That question I posed to Mrs. Grayson was, "how was your relationship with your husband?"

Right away she said, "it was good."

"Is that what you told police?"

"I told them I loved my husband."

"And when they looked at you for his murder, what did you tell them?" She started to become frustrated, "I told them I didn't want him dead."

"You said your relationship with your husband was good. How much time did you spend together say in the course of a week?"

"Plenty."

"Did you notice changes in his moods or behavior?"

"No, not really."

"When is the last time you did something with him outside the home?"

"We ate out before I left to visit my sister."

"Had you ever traveled without him accompanying you before?"

She chose not to answer that one. "What are you getting at," she asked.

"Do you believe he had any reason to take his life?"

"No. I mean we were having some money problems for a while several months back, but Andrew and I managed to pull some money out of the house to take care of things while he found another job."

"So, he recently made a career move."

"Yes, but he was for it."

"Where did you stand with it?"

"He had my support, of course."

"What type of work did your husband do?"

"He was a marketing rep for a local television station."

"And before that?"

"He was a shift manager at Color Tech."

"How long was he there?"

"Look, the police didn't ask all these questions. What does this have to do with my husband slipping in the hot tub and hitting his head?"

"I'm just trying to understand your husband's state of mind at the time of his death. Things that don't seem important often can be. I take it he changed jobs rather frequently."

"Look Andrew was his own person, okay."

"Okay. Did he ever show any signs of depression or make mention of stress being too overwhelming?"

"No."

"Well, that's good. These are important facts that can support your claim of your husband's death being an accident." That seemed to stabilize her a little as I said, "so, there was never any treatment he received pertaining to mental or emotional problems."

She confidently agreed, "absolutely not."

"Well, in order to prove your husband's death was truly an accident, I'm going to need you to allow me access to some of his personal information."

"Like what?"

"Cell phone records, financial information, contact names of people he associated with recently. Those are the important things to look at first to rule out he had any reason for ending his life."

"I see. Well, I can get you that, I guess."

"Very good, and if you don't mind I'd like to take a few measurements while I'm here." I pulled out the tape measure from my left coat pocket, and I saw the surprise sweep over her face when I asked, "where did you first see the body, exactly?"

Her eyes cut down toward the floor. She looked over at the measuring tape I was holding. She appeared confused, but not to the point most people would notice. Her first response to that question was, "he was over on that side near the wall where the stereo was."

I nodded looking at the speakers which were still mounted to the wall saying, "Jensen, nice system. Your husband must have enjoyed music."

"He did."

I stretched the tape holding it in place, measuring the distance across the hot tub. Taking another measurement along the wall she mentioned, I paused questioning the location she had given me without really saying a word. It was more of a sound that I emitted along with a look of concern that made her ask "is something wrong?"

"Maybe. Which way was his body turned in the tub?"

She looked flustered as she spoke, "that way, I believe."

She pointed toward the steps. "So, you actually saw his face upon entering the room."

"No. His back was turned toward me. His face was in the water."

"I'm sorry. I know this must be difficult. Are you certain his head was pointing toward the steps?"

"Yes."

"Was there any blood found in the room?"

Mrs. Grayson appeared cautious as she answered saying, "I didn't see any. He was electrocuted."

"I know, it's just sometimes other injuries are sustained as a result. You mentioned he hit his head?"

Yes. That's what police said when they found him.

Did they determine what he hit his head on?"

"Probably the side of the tub or maybe the stereo. They weren't sure."

"Was the Jacuzzi running when you returned home?

"Yes."

"You're certain of that?"

"Yes, he was floating in it."

I took one more measurement from the wall socket in question to what would have been the waterline in the Jacuzzi.

"And was the stereo still connected to the receptacle when you found him or had it pulled away from it?"

"It was no longer connected. Anymore questions?"

"Not here. Can I take a look at your electrical panel?"

She showed me to the utility room. I flipped several of the breakers testing them, switching most of them back on except for one. I then turned toward Mrs. Grayson asking her if she remembered seeing where I placed my tape measure.

"Last time I saw it you were holding it measuring the hot tub."

"You're right, that's probably where I left it." I excused myself telling her I'd be right back. She, of course, waited for me wondering how much more of her time I was planning on taking.

Returning to the hot tub I checked the wall outlet. It was dead, so was power to the Jacuzzi. As it turned out my tape measure was in my other pocket, but that little test, and the GFCI breakers inside the panel box told me something she didn't share with me. There was virtually no way the hot tub jets functioned without power going to the receptacle. How Mr. Grayson sustained a shock that resulted in death, and the pump pushing the water in the hot tub remained in operation was quite a mystery. The breakers in her panel box would trip quick at the slightest power surge being detected unless they were faulty, and that left little reason for me to believe she was telling me the entire story accurately.

It had been several months since her husband passed, and it was easy to understand sometimes details can be overlooked. The questions I asked her pertaining to exactly where her husband's body was in relation to the stereo and the steps could have confused her.

Maybe she didn't get a good look at her husband before calling police to the scene. I didn't figure that was the case though. Images like the one she had described to me stick vividly in most peoples' minds longer than they wish to have them. My onsite investigation was done at that point, but the digging into Mr. Grayson's demise had only gotten started.

Before leaving Mrs. Grayson's home, I asked when she thought she could get me the information I had requested. She promised to have it to me within forty-eight hours basically, and I had confidence it was high on her agenda. She wanted me to confirm at that point that from what I had seen, and determined made it appear Mr. Grayson's death was an accident. All I could offer her was, "well, the most compelling evidence is no note was left by your husband indicating he chose to take his life. That should be reason enough for the insurance company to reconsider their position, but your problem lies with the determination made by police, I'm guessing." She admitted that was one of the things that concerned police before ruling it a suicide. When I asked her if she believed her husband would have explained his actions in that type of situation, she pressed her lips together tightly before speaking. "You know Andrew never was big on words, and he certainly wasn't much on writing, but I do believe he would've taken the effort to leave some explanation given the chance."

More pieces of the puzzle were now on the board with fewer fitting into place. On my way out the door, I turned to ask Mrs. Grayson one final question after telling her I'd take a look at the coroner's report to see if it could substantiate her belief. "If there's a need to take a second look at the body, would you permit your husband's corpse to undergo additional analysis?"
"Well, that would be impossible."
"Let me guess, you had him cremated."
"Yes. Andrew didn't like closed in spaces, and honestly, that was the cheapest way to handle final arrangements."

I believed her on that one. I had recently looked into the costs surrounding final arrangements for myself, and there was a considerable difference between being buried or burned. I had no intention of re-examining Mr. Grayson's body. The cost to do it far outweighed what I was potentially getting paid on this case, and Fetch wasn't about to help me by doing it. I mainly wanted to know how Mrs. Grayson felt about it. My meeting with Mrs. Grayson lasted longer than I had planned, but all in all the day had shaped out to be eventful.

Chapter 43

Hitting The Streets

I still had another address to check where Rhea lived previously, but I didn't put a great deal of hope in finding a lead there that would amount to much. I had less than an hour before I needed to be back in time to take the kid off Teddy's hands. He worked short days on Saturdays, when he worked them, but I figured I had time to strike this place off my list in my search for the kid's aunt.

The house was easy enough to find, although the neighborhood had changed some since I last ventured through it. Rhea rented there for two years back in 97'. So, this was a cold one for sure. I first knocked on the door of the house next to the one she had rented. The lady there didn't seem interested in answering any questions until I explained why I was looking for the woman that used to live in the house next to her.

People naturally assumed the worst, mainly because they see so much of it on the news, and I wasn't carrying a giant check with me. So, she knew right away I wasn't with Publisher's Clearinghouse. As it turns out, she had two kids herself, and she hadn't been there that long. She was still unsure of which supermarket was closest, and she didn't talk to neighbors that much other than the usual good-bye and hello. She did point at the house across the street mentioning she had seen an old man take out the trash occasionally. She assumed he had been in the neighborhood for a while based solely on his age, I guess, and that was about the extent of the help she was able to give me.

Against my better judgment, I followed the woman's advice, and went across the street to talk to the old guy. I preferred to talk to women when it came to matters like this because guys tended not to know half as much as their female counterparts did about people living around them. Women knew actual dates that people moved, and their reason for leaving in the first place. They even knew details about family crisis affecting their neighbors. Guys on the other hand preferred not to know any of that shit, and if they did they kept it to themselves until they forgot about it altogether. That didn't take long either.

The name on the mailbox read Dauber. The small bit of yard he had in front of the house was weed-ridden, and from the smell of the trash cans it went without saying it was getting close to trash day. I knocked on the door twice and there was no answer. Twice more before giving up and heading toward the steps to leave when I heard the old codger shuffling to the door yelling, "I'm coming, you young punk." It had been a while since anyone referred to me in that fashion. It was refreshing being called that after twenty years even if it was by a man in his early seventies. He opened the door with a friendly grin asking, "what the hell do you want?"

The guy had a great demeanor, just the kind of fellow any P.I. would long to interview. At first, I took him as a no nonsense type of chap, and I said, "don't worry, I'm not here to sell you something."

"That's good, cause I'm not buying it," he barked back. I told him who I was and what I was doing on his front porch and he responded with, "what the hell kind of name is Pepper?"

I proudly informed him it was the name of the best damned investigator in Boston. He shook his head a little not buying what I had told him muttering, "well, what the hell do you need me for?"

"I just need to know if you can tell me anything about the woman I'm looking for. She used to live in that house across the street from you seven years back. Have you been here that long?" He proceeded to tell me he had been there for over twenty years. I heard about where he worked at the time when he bought the place, and the stretch he did in service back during the Korean War. Bringing the guy forward enough to give me some information worth having was the hard part. He would have made an excellent history teacher though.

Trying to bring the old guy back around I said, "the woman I'm looking for probably lived there seven years ago." I gave him a brief description of what she looked like, early twenties, slender, dark brown hair, shoulder length, drove a Maxima I believe. Her name was Rhea Fallon at the time."

He looked a little foggy to me as he questioned me saying, "if I did know something about this person would it be against the law for me to share it with you?"

"No. Like I said at first, I'm just an investigator trying to find her so I can reunite her with family."

"Yeah, well how do I know you're not one of those wackos out there like I see on the TV, stalking people and stuff?"

"I guess you'll just have to take my word for it, but I'd be a pretty pathetic stalker if I had lost track of the party I was trying to stalk, and the closest lead I had was an address this old."

I watched him process what I had said, and he had to qualify things with me one last time before spilling his guts telling me everything he knew about the girl I was looking for. "Okay, you're sure I wouldn't be breaking the law by telling you anything?"

"Yes."

"And you're not a pervert or anything, right."

"That's right."

"Okay then."

"Well, what can you tell me?"

He shook his head, and carelessly brushed me off waving his hand in my direction saying, "I can't tell you anything about that girl cause I don't remember seeing her. Seven years is a long time."

He started to drift back in time again to a point before his married years telling me about a girl he met prior to his wife, but I didn't have time for it even if the story revolved around the woman's legs. Evidently, that managed to stick with the old fellow.

Ten minutes, which seemed like thirty, standing there talking to the old fart for nothing. I was disappointed in myself for letting him take up that much of my time. In fact, I wanted that part of my life back. Anything I did with it would have been more productive than that. I could have spent it at a bar enjoying two for one specials, or picketing naked down the sidewalk to help solve the problems of poverty, homeless pets, breast cancer and world hunger. He was still talking as I walked off the porch, but he stopped right in the middle of what he was saying, asking if I'd mind carrying his trash down to the curb for him. I just looked at him.

"Yeah, I'll get it. At least one of us can help the other, too bad you couldn't tell me anything worth knowing."

That's when he muttered, "that woman just moved out last year."

I argued my point with him for a third time. "No, it was seven years ago."

The old guy became a little agitated with me claiming, "Rita lived there for twelve years - I think I ought to know."

"Her name was Rhea."

"No, it wasn't. The woman that owned that house was named Rita!"

I knew Rhea didn't own the home she lived in at that address, she rented it. The old guy didn't know who I was looking for, but he knew someone that knew Rhea, apparently.

"Did Rita ever rent that house to anyone?"

"Yeah, she rented the back half of it out after her husband died right up until she sold it. Now, the whole damn neighborhood's gone to pot," he grumbled. I looked at his front yard thinking he had a point there, but I was no landscape expert, and I didn't feel like pushing a mower so I didn't mention it. The snow would take care of it soon enough. That's probably how he saw it.

"Last year, huh?"

"Yeah, is something wrong with your hearing?"

"No, just a little hardheaded at times, that's all."

"Yeah, I knew a guy like that once." He could have been referring to himself, but he started talking about some guy he served with in the Marine Corps, and I knew it was time for me to get those cans to the street, and hit the road in time to pick up the kid. I cut him off asking, "so, where's Rita now?"

"Bought her a place down in Melbourne, Florida." He held up his pointer finger hollering, "wait a minute she sent us something!"

He stepped back inside the house as I totted the smelly garbage to the road. All I needed was a last name to get a hold of her, but the old man did me one better. He stepped back outside holding a brochure in his hand which read *Sunny Dale Retirement Community*. "This is where she's at." There was a number right on the brochure along with the address. I asked if Rita had a last name and he said, "Wilkes." That was all I really needed.

He had discarded the envelope which it came in with the return address, but the old guy gripped the brochure firmly in his hand. It was clear he had no intention of parting with it. I took out my pen jotting down what I needed as he pointed to some of the pictures with a bit of excitement in his voice informing me, "they even handle all the yard work for you."
"Yeah, that's great," I said.

Within minutes, I was back inside my car leaving the neighborhood for good, wondering if I would ever reach that place in life where investing my life savings in something just to avoid trimming grass, and shoveling snow looked pretty good as in his case. The answer was, maybe I was already there cause I didn't do either one of them.

Chapter 44

Art Of Hustling

Cruising down Broadway, I listened to the radio, it was just hours before the next game, and Louie had called to congratulate me on my winning streak, and to check and see if I wanted to up my wagers. The Red Sox were doing well, two more wins made me five hundred dollars better off. In a situation like that I couldn't complain. I was tempted to press my luck even further telling Louie to let it all ride on the next two games, but I didn't want to jinx my team.

It's a fine line you walk when you manage a gambling addiction, and hold a true love for a team. Sometimes, it's like beer and liquor, you should never mix the two. I'm not superstitious mind you, just cautious at times, but so far the kid had brought me luck. I told Louie to let the bet stand as is, and I'd shoot him some more action once they made it to the World Series. Louie came back with, "I can't wait," and he truly meant it. He was a diehard Sox fan too.

It had been well over four hours, and I was certain she was probably driving Teddy crazy at that point. Maybe leaving her with him wasn't the best plan I had ever come up with, but I was just thankful to have someone I could depend on to watch her while I took care of business as best I could under the circumstances. What the hell they were up to God only knows. Teddy knew how to work people better than Joe, and there was no telling what he kid would pick up while hanging out with him. At best, that would be a can of shoe polish and a rag. Teddy wasn't one to stay abreast of child labor laws, much less adhere to them. For all I knew the kid was learning the age old technique of applying the proper amount of polish to some guy's loafer to produce the proper amount of shine. Teddy started in the business when he was younger than her. I didn't picture Kelsey as a shoeshine girl though even though she was a bit of a clean freak in my book.

Pulling up in front of my office, I had no idea what I'd discover. Entering the building, it was safe to say, it was the first time I had ever seen Teddy shine a pair of shoes while singing and moving to the Jitterbug song by, you guessed it, that once popular fade-away 80's duo Wham. Needless to say, it kept Kelsey entertained, his customers seemed to enjoy it too.

A line was starting to form cause he was quite good for and old shine man. Teddy could obviously cut a rug with the best of them all while buffing and brushing. It was what I dubbed a show and shine. Teddy should have charged extra for it, I was amused. Wait, this is Teddy we're talking about, he never missed the chance to make a buck. He was charging for it, that I was certain, right along with the box of candy bars sitting on the table next to his chair. No one left his chair without purchasing one, and they all tipped Teddy for the added performance.

How did Teddy sell those over-priced candy bars you ask? I'll tell you. He had the kid do it for him under the guise of selling candy bars to raise money for her school. This was Teddy at his best. He probably had the kid working on commission, but she was selling those candy bars to anyone that passed. That was partially due to Teddy's fast talking, and the kid's ability to pooch out her bottom lip on cue. It didn't take a genius to figure out the racket these two were running, but I had to admit they were quite good at it.

Let's face it, people tend to trust old shine men and little girls. They were both naturals at the con. They looked like they had worked together since the day the kid was born, and what you should take away from this is you should never buy into what they try to sell you, but the candy bars were looking good since I hadn't taken time to eat lunch.

I complimented Teddy on his footwork, and asked the kid if she missed me. She didn't really answer that though. She just said, "hey, Pepper. Would you like to buy a candy bar?"

"Sure, kid. How much for the hundred thousand dollar bar?"

"For you, it's just three dollars."

I looked at Teddy telling him, "that's highway robbery."

He just shrugged his shoulders as he said, "it's called free enterprise."

"There's nothing free about it. How much for the snickers?"

Kelsey looked at Teddy, and he leaned down whispering something in her ear. That's when she informed me, "that one's $3.50."

She did it without conscience, Teddy must have taught her that.

"That's insane," I said. "I'm not paying that."

"But it's the last one."

Teddy added, "they're going quick. You better move on this while it's still left."

"Maybe you didn't hear me, I'm not paying that much for a candy bar."

Kelsey came back with the line which closed everyone. "But it's for my school."

Teddy chimed in with, "you want her to get an education don't you?"

"Yeah, I'm the one getting schooled here. Do I look like some kind of sucker? Don't answer that."

"Okay, since you are taking care of me for you just $2.00,

that's all."

"You taught her that."

"Hey, I just bought the kid some candy bars. What she charges for them, that's up to her."

"I'm not believing you."

"What?"

"I leave her with you for few hours and…"

"Hey you said don't hustle the kid, not don't teach the kid how to hustle."

I shook my head, then reached in my pocket pulling out two one dollar bills. "Give me the snickers kid."

"Well, congratulations. Looks like you reached your goal kid."

Teddy pulled a handful of ones and fives out of his front pocket as he said, "here's the five dollar bonus I promised you for selling them all. You did good." Kelsey stood there looking at Teddy her hand still holding the five.

"Put it in your pocket kid, before he thinks that you don't want it. I'm sure you earned it."

The kid quickly pocketed the five, and she stuck her hand back out waiting for Teddy to give her more money. Teddy gave that look he often gives me of fuzzy forgetfulness as he said, "Oh yeah, you probably want the twenty percent I said was yours."

"It was twenty-five."

"Are you sure about that? I could have sworn we agreed to twenty."

"Nope, it was twenty-five."

"Alright, if you're sure. Let's see that's twenty candy bars at two bucks a piece."

I had just taken a bite of my overpriced snickers bar as I struggled to say, "hey, I thought they were $3.50."

Teddy replied, "only for our special customers." He then laughed as he winked at the kid, and she began laughing right along with him.

I chewed as I tried to speak. "What's that supposed to mean?"

Kelsey told me, "Teddy said you wouldn't buy it if…" Teddy shook his head, and Kelsey stopped without saying another word.

"What's the big secret?"

"If she told you it wouldn't be a secret now would it."

I watched as Teddy peeled off a five and four ones saying, "that makes nine I owe you then."

"Don't let him stiff you kid, he owes you twelve-fifty." The kid looked back at Teddy as I watched him explain, "I wasn't trying to stiff her. I was just testing her that's all."

"Yeah whatever."

On top of the hustle, Teddy also taught her how to play checkers like nobody's fool, and she schooled me on the checkerboard without mercy more than once. It got to where it was no fun playing her whatsoever, but the reasons I gave for not having time to sit down at the checkerboard were real. I had three cases to work, and I wasn't making much headway on them.

Chapter 45

Caring For The Kid

One thing was for sure, the kid needed a bath and a change of clothes, and I needed a break, and some time to work a case. There was only one place that came to mind at that moment. In retrospect, I should have thought harder. I didn't want to do it, but I picked up the phone and dialed the number. Claudia answered, she was surprised to hear the sound of my voice, but surprised was better than livid. So far, so good. I confessed to her, "I need to ask you for a favor. I'm not interrupting you, am I?"

I could hear the sound of her exhale as she started to answer me by asking, "would it matter? What do you want?"

She sounded stern and erotic all at the same time. How she pulled it off left me wondering. There was no turning back now though, I had her on the phone right where I wanted her, and I needed her shower. I calmly explained, "I just need to use your bathtub, if that's alright." That struck her as an odd request as she started to ask what for, but I ended the call without getting into it over the phone as I said, "look, I'm on my way over. So, if it's not too much trouble just have it filled with water when I get there. Alright?" I usually found it best to take the firm approach with her considering her chosen profession. What the hell, she thought of it as honest work. I really can't tell you what I was thinking as I loaded the kid in the car and carried her over to Claudia's place.

Kelsey had to ask me numerous questions on the way there. When she enquired where we were headed I told her "some place where you can take a bath, and change clothes."

She was bold enough to point out I wore the same thing every day. So, why couldn't she? That opened up a long discussion concerning basic hygiene. Kelsey, of course, had her own opinions she felt compelled to share with me. When it came to Claudia she had questions about her as well. Starting with, "what's she look like?"

"She's different," I replied, hoping to leave it at that. What was I supposed to tell her, she was busty, built with legs that went on forever and blonde, redheaded or brunette based on which wig she chose to wear. I don't think so.

"Is she nice?"

Forceful and demanding were words that came to mind when I thought of Claudia, but I answered the kid's question with a question. "Would I be taking you there if she wasn't nice?"

"That's not an answer." The kid was sharp, no doubt. "She's not nice is she?"

I went with my first description of her, "she's different."

"You keep saying that so I know she's not nice. Does she have kids?"

"No. Now, stop asking questions."

"I don't think I'm going to like her."

"Be positive, would you. Teddy was different and you like him."

"Teddy is fun, he does magic tricks and he lets me eat chocolate." I thought to myself Claudia knows tricks, but I didn't dare utter a word regarding that. Claudia's mischievous side usually brought with it lots of pain.

"Let's hope she has chocolate."

Kelsey posed the all-important question, "what if she doesn't?"

That's when I decided to make the turn into the parking lot of the convenience store two blocks north of Claudia's house.

"What do you say we grab a candy bar, how about it?" I had no trouble getting her agreement on that suggestion. As we climbed back in the car I said, "eat it quick kid, we're almost there."

Within less than sixty seconds we pulled up in front of Claudia's place. It appeared normal enough from the outside. Who the hell would've ever guessed a dominatrix lived there? Kelsey's lips were covered with chocolate not to mention her hands. Maybe the candy bar wasn't my best idea. "Come out my side," I told her. She did as instructed leaving me a small partial chocolate handprint on the steering wheel of my Ford Fairlane. I didn't care at that point, I was close to making the handoff.

Claudia opened the door wearing a nurse's outfit holding a sponge in one hand as she said, "I hope you're ready for your bath because the temperature is just right." I stood there reconsidering my actions, and questioning my judgment as the kid peeped around from behind me looking at Claudia dressed in her short nurse's uniform. I heard Kelsey say "oh great," as I looked down at her. Claudia was completely caught off guard as I said, "you heard her kid, grab the sponge and hit the tub. It's straight down that hall on the right."

Claudia stared at me. Her eyes were almost piercing a hole right through my head as she said, "a kid. Two weeks with no phone calls, and this is your idea of an afternoon surprise."

"Look, I've been busy. The kid is just part of the story, but I've got no one else that can watch her. I really need your help on this one." She loved to watch me beg.

"This one is going to cost you," she informed me.

"I'll only be gone a little while, but if I'm not back by tonight, tell her a bedtime story for me. She likes that before she goes to sleep. Claudia gave me a disconcerted look offering up, "she'll be alright. Thanks for dropping by."

I promised to make things up to her as I made a b-line toward my car. Hopefully, she wouldn't hold me to it, but a guy has to do what he has to do in a situation like that. I was just praying she wouldn't force me to be her slave for a week handling all of her house chores. There are worse fates one could suffer though, especially, under Mistress Claudia, but leaving the kid there gave me time to clear my mind a little, and work on finding Rhea, and focus on the Burke case along with what really happened to Mr. Grayson. Let's face it, I had my hands full.

Chapter 46

Information And The Money Shot

I finally managed to reach Rita Wilkes by phone thanks to the help of someone at the Sunny Dale Retirement Community named Gladys. A thirty minute long distance call explaining who I was and who I was searching for left me with one important detail I didn't have previously. Rita Wilkes was Rhea's landlord seven years back, and she spoke highly of the young woman, though now Rhea was in her early thirties. According to her, it appeared Rhea had found her soul-mate since she became engaged to a guy name Gordon Haskins while living there in the back half of Rita's house on Pearl Street.

I thanked her for the information, and she wished me luck in finding her former tenant telling me to say hello for her when I did. Then, she wanted me to update her on how her old neighbors were doing. I just informed her Mr. Dauber said the neighborhood has all gone to pot. She tried to hit me with a barrage of questions starting with what color her old house was now, and whether or not the Peterson's had fixed up their place or taken down the walnut tree next to her old driveway. None of that mattered to me though. I just told her Mr. Dauber was thinking seriously about venturing down to Florida to see her before saying, "oh, and I gotta go." The sound she heard next was the click from me hanging up. She seemed like a nice lady, and I hated to do it, but I also couldn't afford the long distance rate AT&T was charging me. Like I said though, she was helpful. So, in the end the call was worth it.

My investigation now took an immediate shift. I was now looking for Rhea Haskins in addition to Rhea Fallon. From what Mrs. Wilkes told me, Rhea's future husband planned on taking a job in Maryland, and that seemed as good a place to start as any. I still planned on interviewing her former employer, but there was the chance I might get lucky and locate her without their help. Truthfully, I was just relieved to talk to someone that actually knew her other than Eddie.

I began doing an online records search for Kelsey's aunt under both names. Within minutes of me doing so a call came in, it was Mrs. Burke. She informed me her husband claimed he had to go into the office for a while and she planned on going there to tail him herself. I told her I wouldn't recommend it, and that I already had some pictures being developed that would address all of her concerns. I lied on that one as I pulled out the GPS locater, and she grilled me on details. Seeing where Mr. Burke's car was at that moment I could tell she wouldn't be happy with what she found when she arrived at his office.

I promised her I'd have what she asked for in less than twenty-four hours, and she informed me I'd better or else I was fired. She had to take it out on someone. It might as well have been a detective few people cared about. Thing was, I never took it personal. She was upset and I understood. I guess, I was just use to the abuse at that point and wealthy women knew how to dish it out.

I didn't bother to tell Mrs. Burke where her husband was or what he was up to at that very moment. I just chose to drive there myself, and grab a few pictures of him and his girlfriend so I could close the case and get paid. She had no idea I had his car tagged to begin with, and I wasn't sharing that information with her. The only negative was she was now pissed-off from being put-off, and her patience was nonexistent. Reality was, I needed the rest of her money just to meet expenses along with what I had already won from the bets I'd placed with Louie. Maybe I should have doubled down with him on the last two games of the season. There's nothing like winning a parlay to help see a guy through a tough holiday season.

I followed Burke from his secretary's apartment to another restaurant. The contact between them at the table was kept to a semiprofessional level. Still, there was brief touching and long looks with shared eye contact between them that would suggest something else existed in their relationship. Looks like that would make most people feel a little uncomfortable unless they were fairly intimate with one another, and I knew without question Burke had already been there and done that. I could only guess at what was going on under the table, but I had a pretty good imagination. Burke looked a little too happy when the waiter left with the desert tray. He didn't even bother to take a look at the cheesecake, and he was the kind of guy that liked to indulge himself.

I sat there munching on what was left of a stale bagel with a clear picture through a photo lens of what it was like on the other side. Even left unmagnified it was better than my world. Sitting there monitoring them, I rolled different descriptions through my mind of what to call this case to give it a sense of flare. The Burke case just didn't quite seem ample to describe it. I leaned more toward dubbing it the case of the sultry secretary, and her well-to- do middle-age employer with a high dollar money grubbing wife of seventeen years. That was too long though, and too wordy. I'd never manage to get all that written on the folder label.

That's when I opted for calling it the high-end affair, less descriptive but classy. Knowing Mrs. Burke as I did, she would've preferred I kept it that way.

The check finally came, and Burke paid it leaving plenty of tip just to impress his female companion. The waiter had to like that part, the guy probably made more money than I did just for keeping his mouth shut. They exited the restaurant heading in separate directions, but still communicating with one another as they walked toward their cars. I continued surveillance following her for a change, mainly cause the scenery was better in my eyes. It didn't matter, Burke was drawn to her like a magnet. I was banking on them rendezvousing again somewhere. If they didn't, I'd take what I had and give it to Mrs. Burke so she could stick it to her soon-to-be ex-husband.

Mr. Burke's secretary made a quick stop to get gas, and then she returned to her place of work parking her car in the rear of the building. Burke's car was nowhere in sight when I arrived, but that wasn't surprising. He usually parked in the parking garage, and there was no reason to believe that night would be any different. That's how he managed to keep the paint on his Mercedes in pristine condition. I had to check it out though just to make sure I wasn't wasting my time there. I also needed my locater back if he was there, and that seemed like the perfect time to get it. I was stunned to find he wasn't there yet, but patience is a real virtue in this business.

Choosing a place to park on the third level, I sat there waiting to take the money shot. Just when I thought he wasn't going to show, I saw him on the adjacent street next to his office building. He was heading straight for his usual parking space. The guy never disappointed me which is more than I could say for his wife in that case.

Mr. Burke had a spring in his step as he left his vehicle. Who wouldn't? He had a nice car, a cushy job, and a hot secretary that was into him. He also had Mrs. Burke he told lies to, but there was just something about the guy that made you feel like he had something worth living for, at that moment it was his secretary. Just like clockwork and gravity, within less than thirty minutes they were back together at his office. What took place behind the glass, and louvered blinds certainly wasn't business as usual. If it was, I needed to get a job there instead of sitting in the cold flying solo in the Fairlane aiming my camera lens through the windshield at the upper level window of a commercial building photographing someone else's gratification moment.

It was heated and tawdry, and acrobatic at times. I saw everything from shirts to a skirt flying through the air as if they were being tossed by jugglers, and the mess that was made in the office when his secretary swept the papers off of Mr. Burke's desk onto the floor was sure to piss-off the janitor. I had to give them one thing though, they had serious passion for what they did there. They even made a few copies on the copy machine to prove it.

One things for certain, I damn sure got the money shot. Lester was going to like this set of prints. I think that's what he liked most about his job, that and the cheap high he got from working around the chemicals.

It was hard to feel sorry for a guy like Mr. Burke, but somehow I did. I couldn't explain it. He had life better than me in many ways, but I didn't have to worry about answering to Mrs. Burke, and I knew she was going to rake him over the coals with what I was about to hand her. Well, that will teach him. It was sure to be an expensive lesson. That's what I thought as I pulled out of the parking garage, that, and perhaps I should look into hiring a secretary - just to help me manage some of the paperwork that goes along with this business. You know what I mean.

I left Blondie and Mr. Burke to their fun, and dropped the film off with Lester. I told him to put a rush on it, and no mishaps this time. The whole case was in his hands, literally. He liked it when the pressure was on, I could tell. He promised my one hour turnaround, and assured me there would be no problems this time, and I believed him.

Chapter 47

Horror Movies And Sex Pictures

When I finally returned to check on Kelsey and Claudia, I found the two of them watching a horror movie munching on popcorn, and eating ice cream. Hearing the bloodcurdling screams, I took one look at the television. It was a bit traumatizing to watch, even for me. "What the hell is that?"

Claudia responded, "just a scary movie. It's girl's night, this is what we do," as if that made it okay.

From what I could see on the screen, it looked like a bloody sleepover at a sorority house. All I can say is thank God Claudia didn't have on her schoolgirl uniform. Kelsey's eyes were glued to the screen, and her face was half-filled with terror. The other half seemed glad to see me when I asked, "you doing alright, kid?"

She responded with "yeah, we're just watching movies."

I asked Claudia if she thought that was the best thing for the kid to watch, and she informed me she had things under control. "She probably sees worse things hanging out with you."

I couldn't argue that, nor wouldn't with Mistress Claudia. I was just thankful she wasn't watching something out of Claudia's private movie collection cause I had seen one or two, and they left me scarred. "We're about to do toenails, care to join us?" Claudia had that sarcastic tone in her voice mixed with seduction. She had a way about her that brought her plenty of business. She could tell you to go get bent, and make it sound erotic in a dominant, stern kind of way, I had to give it to her.

"No. I was just checking in to make sure everything was going okay. If it's not too much trouble, do you think you can keep her overnight? I can pick her up tomorrow evening."

"That's fine," she informed me. "We're going shopping." I didn't ask what for. Truth is I didn't want to know, but the kid needed clothes, and that sounded good to me. I had expected Claudia to shove the kid out the door the minute I pulled up in the driveway, but she managed to surprise me once again, this time with mothering instincts. I didn't even have to pay her to provide them either, unlike some of her regular clients, but we won't go into their sorted secrets.

"See you tomorrow kid."

Kelsey responded with, "okay," never turning away from the television. I could tell the kid really missed me. It was probably pure torture for her being stuck there with the not so nice lady she called Miss Claudia, but it was better than doing another night of surveillance, and word-find puzzles. That, I was sure of.

Claudia told her to pick out a nail polish as she placed her hand on my chest asking me, "is that all you wanted?" She made me want to say no, but I nodded my head yes, and that's when she pulled open the door pushing her hand firmly against me shoving me out into the cold. The words she left me with were, "come back when you're ready." She closed the door, and I stared at it for a second or two before coming to my senses, and hopping my ass in the car in order to take care of business.

That evening I returned to pick up the pictures I had promised to deliver to Mrs. Burke. Lester spotted me as soon as I walked in. He raised his chin a little which meant I've got what you want, and then he followed the head gesture with a wink as he walked over to the counter. That meant he liked what he saw. Hey, detectives are good at finding out other peoples secrets, and documenting them with tangible proof, keeping them from their photo techs - well, that's another story.

Lester pulled out a large white envelope with the word "HOLD" written on it in all caps. Reaching inside pulling out two packets of pictures labeled 'A' and 'B', he pointed to one of the packets placing his finger directly on it as he said, "this one is pretty hot by the way. I made double prints for you just in case you needed to keep a copy for your records." Then he gave me that deliberate head nod which expressed you know what I mean. "There's no extra charge for that by the way, and here's your extra film I promised." I went to thank him and he told me, "don't mention it. The pleasure was all mine." To be honest, sometimes I felt Lester enjoyed his job way to damn much. As I went to pay him he couldn't help but ask, "so, who's the blonde in the pictures, anyway." I never answered questions like that, truthfully anyway. Just as I went to respond he held up his hand saying, "no. That's okay, forget I asked. It's probably best I don't know."

"Yes it is," I agreed. Lester and I had that conversation on a regular basis it seemed. He handed me my change which I never bothered to count saying, "until next time my friend," and with that I was out the door.

Chapter 48

One Step Closer To Closing A Case

I poured over everything I could find on Rhea Haskins aka Rhea Fallon, expecting to get a call from Mrs. Burke which never came, but I knew for certain she'd be calling first thing in the morning after her husband went to work. I figured her timing would be perfect right when I was in the middle of talking to Detective Langford about Mr. Grayson's death. Or, maybe while I was interviewing Rhea's former employer. I couldn't help that though.

What I did find out about the kid's aunt could fill a mini shot-glass. It turns out she was married for three years to this Gordon guy, but the marriage didn't last. Due to irreconcilable differences the couple filed for divorce in January of 2001 in the state of Connecticut. There were also no kids resulting from that marriage, and Rhea had taken her former name back. Who could really blame her on that one? I don't know too many woman that would have signed on to be Mrs. Gordon Haskins in the first place based solely on the guy's name. The leads kind of ran cold after discovering that. It seemed I was going to have to push a little further toward the end of the earth to find her, at least outside of New England.

I looked at my watch after rubbing my eyes feeling this missing person case could go on forever. I had to try and remain positive though both for myself, and for the kid's sake. I stretched sitting there in my chair thinking how much I had missed the feel of the sofa in the other room. Knowing how late it was, and what I had ahead of me, I decided to take advantage of it.

My hopes certainly weren't high when I entered the reception area at the Humphrey and Doyle accounting firm. The lobby was posh and colonial looking, complete with antique furnishings and elegant trim moldings. It was where the money came to have their numbers crunched, and I was there without an appointment. I checked in with the girl at the front desk, Tara was her name, and she was friendly. When I told her why I was there, she appeared puzzled as she tried to determine who could best help me. She had never met Rhea, but the name she said sounded familiar to her. She offered me coffee, and I took her up on it. She pointed to some pastries informing me they were free, and she encouraged me to help myself. I did just that before taking a seat in the leather chair as I waited on her to return with the coffee, thinking this place isn't half bad. In my opinion it was better than Best Western.

I was just about to go for seconds when a man wearing an expensive suit walked out to greet me. He addressed me by name saying, "I'm Mr. Fuller. I understand you are trying to locate Miss Fallon. Is that correct?"

I responded, "yes, I am. Do you think you can help me?" He was cordial in nature motioning with his arm as he turned slightly.

"Let's see, please join me in here where we can talk." He ushered me into a nearby conference room. I looked the place over comparing it to my office. Things at Humphrey and Doyle were done up on a different scale, let's just leave it at that.

Mr. Fuller proceeded to ask a few questions of his own, mostly pertaining to why I was looking for his former employee. The fact that I was a private investigator seemed to intrigue him. "You know, I don't believe I've ever met a P.I. in person, and I'm certain we don't have one here at the firm as our client. That must be a very interesting profession," he said in a questioning manner.

"It has its moments, but I don't have an office like this." It was a compliment, and he took it humbly.

"I'm sure you don't need it. This is just what our clients have come to expect, and we work hard around here to keep them, thank you though. Who does your taxes, if you don't mind my asking?"

"I don't mind. I've been using the same guy for years over off of Washington, but the reason I'm here is to find Rhea Fallon. Can you tell me where she went after leaving here?"

"Rhea was looking at a taking a job in New York when she left us. I hated to see her go, but she was planning to get married, and her husband was looking to leave Boston as I recall."

"I don't think she ever made it to New York. I did find an old address she lived at in Connecticut."

New York was the biggest haystack of all, and I didn't want to have to wade through it. Fuller thought a moment before saying, "hang on." He leaned forward in his chair and reached for the speakerphone in the center of the conference table. Pressing the intercom button he paged his secretary, "Elizabeth, pull Rhea Fallon's personnel folder for me." She told him she'd be happy to as I looked across the table at him. He said, "I just want to check something. Roughly, two years ago I believe someone called asking us to verify her employment with us. The call had to be returned and either Elizabeth or I handled it. So, I'm pretty sure we may have the name of the company or even a contact number to reach them."

"That would be great if you did."

"I think it was a publishing firm. I'm really not sure."

"Well, I appreciate you checking."

"Absolutely. You said her mother is now in a nursing facility?"

"That's correct."

"Well, when you do find her, please tell her we'd love to have her back here should she need to be close to her mother."

"I'll do that."

Elizabeth brought him the file, and Fuller paged through it. I could tell based on his eye movement he was a fast reader, and he had found what he was looking for. "Here it is," he announced. "The name of the company is Fountain Press. I'll have Elizabeth write down their number for you."

It was the best encounter I ever had with a high priced accountant that charged people out the wazoo for his tabulation services. Fuller made mention as I thanked him, "if you really want to thank me, let us handle your tax preparation. I'm sure there's not a deduction that we would overlook for you."

I just shook his hand telling him, "when the time comes." He could take that any way he chose, but I couldn't afford Humphrey and Doyle. I don't know what he was on. I'd have had to take out a loan just to pay them to tell me how much to handover to the state and IRS. I'd need every deduction in the tax code just to cover their fees, but Mr. Fuller was helpful, and I felt I was one step closer to finding Rhea when his assistant handed me the number to Fountain Press.

On my way out, Tara enquired if I had received the assistance I came for, and I simply told her, "yes, thanks to you and Mr. Fuller. Mind if I grab another scone?" She was all smiles informing me that's what they're there for. She then offered to get me some juice to wash it down with, but

I couldn't put her out like that. I just said, "coffee will do, one cream, one sugar." Yeah, I liked the place. Beats me why Rhea ever left it to begin with, and I truly didn't want to wish Tara farewell, but I had work to do.

It was 10:13 a.m. when I phoned Fountain Press. The lady that answered the phone confirmed Rhea was in fact employed there by patching me through to her extension. I had high hopes at that point, but I ended up with a recording of Rhea's pleasant voice explaining she was out of the office, and wouldn't be returning for the rest of the week. It then directed me to a woman name Becky Goldstein if the nature of my call was an emergency.

Call me negative, but I didn't think Becky Goldstein would be willing to help me out on this one. It looked like the kid was going to have to keep her day jobs, and I was going to keep on trying to reach her aunt possibly next week. If she had a personal phone it was unlisted, but I was betting a cell was all she carried. That made her work phone critical to me getting hold of her, but the good news was she was alive, and presumably well when she recorded her voicemail message. I still didn't know how she would take the news I had for her, but Eddie seemed confident Rhea would do what was necessary. That was a lot to lay on someone though, but what choice did I have. For the meantime though, that message would have to wait to be delivered.

Chapter 49

Concerns In This Business

Mrs. Burke still hadn't called which I found somewhat odd as the afternoon approached, but I had been trying to reach Detective Langford by phone off and on all morning. It's possible I missed her call as a result, but she had my cell number, and she wasn't afraid to use it. In a situation like that you worry about the silly stuff like what if something happened to her. What if her and Mr. Burke had it out when he got home that evening? What if she felt she no longer needed the pictures to prove his infidelity to the court or pressure him into giving her everything she demanded in the divorce? What if I don't get paid for all the hours, gas and aggravation on this one? All I know for sure is the "what ifs" in life will kill you.

Those concerns were soon put to rest though once I managed to get the detective on the phone. I had barely made it known who I was, and what I was calling about when Mrs. Burke chose to dial my cell number. I watched my phone buzz as Langford gave me some details of what he had found at the scene. He was working from memory, but his was quite good cause I was looking at the actual report in front of me. "So, you're trying to determine if the insurance company should pay the claim?"

"That's right. There's a suicide clause in his life insurance policy." Langford admitted he had seen that. He had obviously conducted a fairly thorough investigation into the Grayson's finances searching for motive in the case of murder. I would have expected nothing less. The phone stopped, and then thirty seconds later it started buzzing again. I didn't want to lose Langford. He was too hard to get on the phone to start with, and I needed to know where he really stood on the case.

"What was your take when you first arrived?"

"Honestly, it looked as though he did it or someone did him in. I immediately looked at his wife, that's standard. I'm sure you know that, but she had an alibi which checked out."

Against better judgment, I placed my hand over the phone as I listen to Langford answer my question. That's when I chose to take Mrs. Burke's call on my cell phone. I tried to explain I was on the other line, but she was talking over me. Making no headway there, I switched phones asking Langford, "any concerns about the timeline?"

"Well yeah, but it couldn't have been off by two days, and that's when his wife returned home. We verified that with the airport."

"Did anything lead you to believe she would want him dead?"

Mrs. Burke overheard the tail-end of my question to the detective and she responded, "I don't want him dead. I want him paying me alimony for as long as he lives."

I tried to listen to Langford as I directed my comments to Mrs. Burke. "Look, I'm going to have to call you back, alright." They both heard me say that and Langford responded with, "sure." I thought I was about to lose him, and I wasn't done with him yet. What Mrs. Burke said, I really can't say, but some of it was rather unladylike. She got the message though as I hung up on her while trying to explain to Langford that comment was directed at someone else.

The detective glossed over some statements made by Mrs. Grayson. A few of them seemed revealing in a way.

When I asked, "what did your gut tell you?"

He replied, "I didn't like it, but we had no other suspects.

No one saw anyone entering or exiting the home anywhere near the time of death, and there were no other prints found there except for him and his wife's."

"That parts a little odd isn't it?"

"I'll say. They've been in that house for almost five years. You can't tell me in that time some stray prints haven't ended up being left in that room, and the ones that did remain were minimal."

"Cleaned."

"I'd say wiped down from one end to the other. I've investigated scenes where maids had been employed, and they weren't that spotless."

"What about the other rooms in the house."

"The rest of the house seemed untouched compared to where the hot tub was located. That was one of the reasons it really appeared suspicious, and the way in which this guy went seemed horrific."

"Not a pretty site, huh."

"Never is, but you should have seen the guy. He looked like something right out of a horror movie."

He didn't know it, but I was looking right at one of the pictures he snapped of Mr. Grayson, and I had to agree with that assessment.

"I see."

"I've been a detective for over ten years, and I've never really seen anything like it to be honest."

Langford confessed his investigation turned up no solid proof Mr. Grayson died as a result of an accident. The clean-up piece of it was a giveaway something wasn't right. That one bothered him as much as me. Placement of the body didn't seem right either, but pinning anything on Mrs. Grayson according to the estimated time of death was also impossible taking into count the distance between them at the time.

"Was there anything else that stood out to you during the

investigation?"

"Well, there was a head wound. I'm pretty certain that didn't get there deliberately on his part before he took a dive with the stereo."

"You attribute it to an accident after the shock?"

"I had too. No blood was found at the scene. That meant he had to hit his head in the water."

"Just out of curiosity was the hot tub running when you arrived?"

"No. No it wasn't. Why?"

"Well, I just wanted to make sure the circuit breakers were functioning properly. It's an item of liability determination. Insurance companies are always concerned with it."

"Well, those breakers didn't help him one damn bit."

"Anything else you can tell me about the relationship between husband and wife?"

"Not really. At first she seemed to truly be distraught over what had happened to him. A few days later when we spoke with her she still seemed to be grieving, but once we started questioning certain pieces of evidence in the investigation asking her if she could shed some light on things for us, she became more defensive. We asked her directly if she had tampered with the scene or the body itself, and she denied having anything to do with his death, and she was adamant she simply found him like that."

"I take it you believed her."

"We didn't have a case against her for murder, just clean-up. Why she did it, if she did it, I don't know, but a lot of pieces just didn't fit into place on that one."

"Can you say what those pieces were?"

"Not really, but the guy had to commit suicide. There was no need for him to touch the stereo. It could have easily been operated using the remote control, and where it was located on the wall made it difficult to reach while standing inside the hot tub."

Langford made no mention of what was found in Mr. Grayson's nose, but he did say he had a history of substance abuse that had cost him a job previously, and it appeared he was battling the addiction again prior to his death. "Some of the Grayson's financial problems stemmed from that," he added. "It was clear the guy was under stress," Langford said. "He was facing some problems on his new job as well." That was all he said regarding that.

When I asked him to explain, he told me he didn't have time to go into it. I believed him, but I also felt he didn't care to elaborate any further. That case was one he preferred not to think about, and that's how my call ended with him. He didn't ask for me to share any information with him that I uncovered about the case going forward. He didn't expect me to dig that deep, and find anything new that would answer any questions for him.

I took it as far as he was concerned the case was closed after being thoroughly investigated. The conclusion he reached was logical. The body nor the scene itself was remotely in the same condition it was five months earlier. I couldn't complain though, he had given me as much as I had hoped for, and when you see no way for something to be accidental, you can't rule it that way because it's convenient to do so.

Truthfully, I felt he had no intention of rendering that determination simply to prevent Mrs. Grayson from collecting life insurance proceeds based on her husband's death. That was just how the cookie crumbled as Willard used to say.

I could see where Langford stood in the investigation, and why he deemed the thing a suicide. I had taken the measurements myself. Shit didn't add up. The crime scene was too clean for it to be an accident, and something was definitely out of place. The unusual burns on the body Langford didn't go into heavily. He didn't want to discuss something no one was able to explain.

It appeared Mr. Grayson was alone at the time, and the only way to get that stereo in the Jacuzzi with him was for him to put it there. He had to rule out the wife as being a murder suspect because of the plane ticket she had in her possession, and the fact that her sister corroborated her story, but that all came down to time of death.

Chapter 50

Wrapping Up Cases Seldom Came Easy

I was still waiting for the items I had requested from Mrs. Grayson. I would have them soon enough, but Mrs. Burke became my priority after talking to Langford. She was a bit ill-tempered I could tell just before I got off the phone with her, but I was certain she would agree to meet me as soon as I could arrange to see her just get her hands on those pictures.

She answered on the first ring, and that was a dead giveaway she was eager to get down to business. After confirming I had what she wanted she pressed me for a time when we could meet at my office, and I told her, now was as good a time as any. She swore she'd be there in thirty minutes, and she was. The exchange was made, and I was fifteen hundred better off than I was as a result of taking her case. Her tone changed a little as she looked at several pictures of her husband holding his secretary. The pictures themselves were revealing enough. She didn't need to hear the recording. I didn't even bother mentioning it to her at first, but I told her as she turned to leave if her attorney needed more proof, it existed. In the meantime, I told her I'd make sure to hold onto it.

She nodded giving me a final "thank you," before walking out of my office.

Those pictures made an impression on her. The events she envisioned were now made real to her. She didn't seem so full of fire and venom after seeing them. No tears fell on them and no vocal outbursts were heard. What was going through her mind as she carried them next to her chest walking down the hall toward the elevator was anybody's guess. I certainly don't know, I'm no psychologist. I'm just a guy that snaps pictures of people doing what they shouldn't, and sometimes I'm the guy that finds proof that people snap. Either way, I placed the money in my pocket watching the door close as she left knowing that was the end of the high-end affair case. I had spared Mrs. Burke from seeing the most explicit photographs. I had left them in the folder cause I felt it was the right thing. That's how it is in this business, a P.I. with a moral code carries a little weight around with him that doesn't show on the exterior, but I seldom lost sleep over that, if you know what I mean.

It was well after lunch and time to pick up the kid. Claudia and Kelsey had spent a good deal of time together. They seemed as though they clicked in a lot of ways even though Claudia was no kid person by any stretch. She was good at giving orders though, and Kelsey pretty much listened to her. Hell, practically everyone did except for me, and that's what kept things interesting between us. Mistress Claudia knew how to define boundaries if nothing else, and Kelsey tested limits. It was obviously a growing experience for both of them, and to think I was the one that provided them with that opportunity. That's not to say they didn't have fun together because they did, but neither one of them pretended they couldn't wait to see one another again though, and that's just how things were between them.

Sadly, she was the only female the kid really spent any time with, and I wasn't sure that was a good thing, but my choices were limited for the time being. When she climbed in the car I asked her how things went, and she gave me a thumbs up, so, I assumed it was good.

Curiosity got the best of the kid though as I backed out onto the street and she said, "when I grow up I might be a police lady like Miss Claudia, or maybe a nurse. Which one is she?" I prayed at that point she hadn't seen Claudia's cop outfit, cause I had, and it was more revealing than her nurse uniform. "What are you talking about kid?"

"She has pink handcuffs and they're fuzzy. I like them," she added.

"You didn't mess with them, did you?"

"No she doesn't like it when you touch her stuff."

"I know. That's good," I said somewhat relieved.

Kelsey kind of looked at me noticing the inflexion in my voice change some. Then she informed me, "she told me not to play with them cause they were for bad boys, and girls, but I think she's a nurse too though. What do you think?"

"I think she does a lot of undercover work kid. What do say to a milkshake, I'm buying?"

"Sure."

Chapter 51

Discovering The Truth

The next few days I spent focused entirely on the Grayson case. Langford was right about Andrew Grayson's troubles at work. Prior to his death he was about to be handed a termination notice for failure to take a pee-test and several days of unexcused work absence. His wife had provided most of what I asked for, and their finances did show Andrew had an expensive habit. She never bothered to mention anything about his pathway to recovery, or the legal fees they incurred resulting from an accident he had while being under the influence of a controlled substance.

Delores Grayson had described her relationship with her husband as being good, but it didn't show on paper. A sizeable check cut to a family law attorney made it clear that at one point divorce was on the table for the two of them, but that was six months prior to Andrew's death. Delores had chosen to stick it out, and give him another chance, but obviously hindsight shows that decision didn't turn out so well for the two of them.

I called Fetch finding him in class conducting an experiment of some sort. He was studying the effect of temperature variations on the body, a project that was sure to get him the A on his thesis paper, and get me the answers I was looking for. Don't ask me what he was using as a test subject. I didn't ask. He had plenty of access to John and Jane Doe though, but knowing Fetch it was probably a donor cadaver.

"So, what can you tell me?"

"Well, based on average weight of the body, and water temp being room at the time of discovery, your timeline could vary by as much as 48 hours."

"How much time would it take to freeze and unthaw?"

"That part is easy, freezing it takes less than a few hours, unthawing can be done in under one with adequate hot water applied to the skin."

Now it made sense even to me. Andrew Grayson had three types of burns present on his skin, and all of them weren't visible to investigators at the scene since the body was covered with water. Fetch pointed out, "the only way your guy ended up with those burns was to go from one extreme to another, and quick."

"Sometimes you're hot, and sometimes you're cold Fetch, but this time you are on fire."

"I hate to say it, but it looks like your guy was murdered, but you already knew that didn't you."

"I had my suspicions."

"Yeah, well now you know. Say, let me know how it turns out."

"Yeah, I appreciate you doing that for me."

"No problem, I needed to conduct the experiment anyway."

"How's that?"

"It made a great topic for my research paper."

"Really? Who would've ever thought you could major in dead people?"

"I know. Isn't it great?"

"Don't get too excited. I run up on plenty of them, and so do you."

"Well, in my experience, the list keeps growing. I gotta go Pepper. It's my turn to present."

"Good luck killer."

The burns on Andrew Grayson's body were from the shock he sustained when his wife placed the stereo in the hot tub with him. How did I know she did it? The other two sets of burns resulted from the skin being exposed to ice for a prolonged period of time, and also coming in direct contact with boiling water. Those were the extremes Fetch was referring to, and I knew of no way Andrew Grayson could have done all that to himself, plus the added head injury.

There was only one person that would have benefited from throwing off the timeline intentionally, and I knew her personally. How do you prove that simply from photos taken before the body was destroyed? That's the real question. It would be hard to prove in court, but the key was the ability to alter the timeline by that much simply through the use of H_2O in two different states. The fact that the body was submerged in it at the time the body was found made it easy to conceal. Andrew's body could have been washed, and rinsed repeatedly and officials would never know. The absence of clothing being present on the body took away any evidence associated with blood-spatter.

Let's face it, there are few places a body can be found in the buff, and it not draw too much attention. Mrs. Grayson had found one such place in her house, and that's where she put her husband's body. She went to the trouble of wiping the place down to get rid of any evidence that might point to something other than suicide, or accident, but she hadn't clearly read the terms of her husband's insurance policy at that point. I knew that when she first entered my office. If she had, maybe she would have done things differently, but my guess was it wasn't planned out well. She was covering her tracks after something went wrong between them.

My guess was she came home and found out Andrew was using again. Maybe she knew before she left. Perhaps she had given him an ultimatum, and the trip to visit her sister was a final step or the start of a trial separation. Needless to say, things were not good between them.

Phone records didn't reveal calls to other women, but contact between them was almost nonexistent. Days would go by without so much as a two minute phone call being shared between husband and wife, but some numbers showed up more than others. They also coincided with his relapse into drug use. Calling just to check out the theory one of those numbers belonged to his dealer, the guy that kept the Grayson's underwater financially.

Maybe the phone records were where she first noticed he was back at it again. My bet was it was the money he constantly drew out of the bank in large cash increments. Something came to a head five months ago though when she returned home, and whatever it was that struck Mr. Grayson's head was solid. It probably landed there in the heat of anger, but I didn't figure it to be premeditated.

Thinking about it most of that afternoon, I became certain something between them escalated, and Mrs. Grayson physically lashed out at her husband without even thinking. Her words to me when I first interviewed her were, "she told police she didn't want him dead." That, I believed, was an honest statement on her part. She probably assumed she had killed him by accident as soon as she hit him in the head with something hard. Whatever she clubbed him with left an impression on him, and she was left with three choices at that point. She could admit to killing him during a heated argument, and face criminal charges, or she could stage things to make it look like an accident and maintain her innocence telling police she just found him like that. Her only other option was frame someone else for it and call for an ambulance after disposing of the murder weapon. That would be a great deal more difficult.

All I can say is she made the wrong call when she walked through my door to hire me to help her rule the death something other than suicide. I didn't like where I stood at that point, but I couldn't change that. All I could do was what I saw as right given the evidence.

The truth was he probably would have died from the head wound, but she acted fast in a panic, and actually did kill him by electrocuting him. All it took to make it a case the prosecutor would pursue was to place her there with the body at the time of death. Whatever she hit him with wasn't that important. Proving she altered the crime scene to cover her tracks was. Any jury hearing that would most likely find her guilty since electric shock was the cause of death, and she would've had to have a hand in it. Joe was right. She snapped, and she couldn't take her actions back, but she desperately wanted the insurance money.

Andrew Grayson had put his wife in a tight financial squeeze when he was alive, and after he died. I knew a great deal more about him now, and I can't say I had a fondness for him or his wife. She was my client though, and I owed it to Andrew Grayson to see to it no one profited from killing him.

I really didn't want to make the call to Langford, and I felt what I had uncovered shouldn't be shared over the phone with my client. There was little satisfaction I gained from this case other than solving the riddle of three different burns on one body covered with water. I couldn't have done it without Fetch of course, but I had figured it out, and it was time to make Mrs. Grayson aware. That's why I drove over to her house. It was important to see her face to face when I explained what really happened five months earlier.

Chapter 52

The Science of Murder

She met me at the door, and she could tell something was wrong. She noticed that almost as soon as she greeted me. I didn't allow her to say too much before telling her I had something important to address with her. I started off with, "I know without question from your financial records, and your husband's phone records, things weren't that good between the two of you, even though you told me they were earlier this week."

"And?"

There was tension in the air, I believe she held her breath at first as I said, "I know what happened concerning your husband's death, and unfortunately what started out as an accident ended up becoming something much worse."

Looking into her eyes I saw fear. I stared at her not uttering another word just long enough to force her to say, "I don't know what you're talking about." She played it innocent, and calm as she could, but the pitch of her voice was unsteady, and higher than it normally was.

"Well, let me explain it to you, and perhaps you'll understand a little more about how science works. There was a study done recently comparing temperature extremes on the body. The testing in that study produced burns exactly like the ones your husband had on his body. The other significant discovery was by freezing the body or bringing the outer part of it to a frozen state, and rapidly unthawing it using scolding hot water, not only were two different types of burns produced, but the internal organs like the liver which is used to determine the time of death in many cases also suffered a change in temp. It actually changed so much it could throw off the time of death by two days or more. Does that sound significant to you?"

She broke eye contact with me saying, "that's very interesting. I didn't take you for Bill Nye the science guy though. I guess this means you don't think my husband's death was an accident."

"I don't think you killed your husband, intentionally. You as much as told police that. I'm almost certain whatever happened causing him to sustain a head injury was probably never planned. The stereo along with his body finding its' way in the hot tub was just a cover up. It's also what killed him. Technically, I'm sure it was all an accident and perhaps that's what you should tell police."

"And why would I do that?"

"Because manslaughter and murder carry two different sentences. The latter one could cost you your life, and I'd hate to see it happen, but maybe you should level with police, and get yourself a good attorney because once I turn my report in to Detective Langford, I'm certain they are going to wish to interview you again, and this time they'll push for a polygraph."

She looked doubtful and hesitant to speak.

So, I gave it to her straight, "don't think for a second you would pass. Explain to police how it happened, and take the deal they give you for the guilty plea, cause you are never going to see that money from the insurance company."

"Why are you telling me this?"

"You put me onto the case. You're my client, consider it professional courtesy, but I'll have to let them know by tomorrow afternoon if you haven't turned yourself in."

"You don't have to tell them anything."

"Yes. I do."

"Why? I mean, it's not going to bring Andrew back."

"No. You're right there, but I already carry too many

secrets around with me. That one would be too much to tote, I'm afraid."

There was a long silence. She was upset, but the tears had not formed yet. Breaking rule number two, I sincerely told her, "I'm sorry Mrs. Grayson. I had hoped this one would end much better than it did."

I left her standing in her doorway with much more than money weighing on her thoughts as I turned to walk back toward my car. I had doubts she'd take my advice, but I had given her fair warning. A smart P.I. would have gone straight to Langford, maybe even not taken the case to start with, but I didn't always fall in that category unfortunately. The clock was ticking though for Mrs. Grayson. She had to decide to cut a deal, or run, or find some way to keep me from informing police. I preferred not to consider that last option, but it was something I was certain would go through her head at some point no matter what her choice was.

You might be thinking you're crazy Pepper. You don't confront a murder suspect like that, and walk away. They could do anything at that point including kill you. You would be right in thinking so. People become most dangerous when they're cornered. In times like that they do things without giving it a great deal of thought cause there's not much time to think, like in Mr. Grayson's murder.

As trusting a soul as I am, I planned not only to watch her from a distance, but to also listen to her just to gain some idea of what she would do. Call me the ultimate optimist, I just happened to believe Mrs. Grayson would make the right call this time. I was banking on her understanding it was in her best interest I guess.

Sitting in my car, I observed her house, waiting to see

what she would do next. From a comfortable distance using an amplified mic, I listened in on what was taking place inside her home. Her footsteps were heavy, and hasty I'd say, and Mrs. Grayson knew how to slam doors, but within a matter of minutes she picked up the phone to make a panicked call. It was clear she was speaking to her sister. She didn't make a full confession, but she laid out some of the critical talking points of our most recent conversation for her. "What do you think I should do?" I heard her exclaim, "it was an accident! I don't know what this guy is going to do if I don't go to the police. Maybe I should call Harvey."

Harvey Wiseman was her attorney. It sounded like a good move to make on her part. Greenberg and Wiseman would cost her an arm and a leg to handle her defense most likely, but they would probably see to it she got off with manslaughter only serving a year or two tops, and that would be for tampering with a crime scene. Knowing what her financial situation was, there was no doubt she'd have to sell the cars, and the house to use what equity she had to cover the cost of her legal defense.

I can't tell you how I felt at that point. My client was guilty of covering up a murder whether or not she was convicted. I just had to focus on the only positive there was. The case was solved, and yours truly wasn't played for a fool by a black widow.

I hated to do the insurance company any favors, but they wouldn't have to worry about paying out those proceeds to Mrs. Grayson. Alternate beneficiaries like his parents were another story though. It was a sad case any way you looked at it, but in the end, Delores Grayson took her sister's advice I guess. She made that call to the attorney she mentioned, and she expressed her desperate need for help. I didn't need to hear anything further, Andrew Grayson and I were square.

Chapter 53

I Found Someone Special

My persistence finally paid off in Kelsey's case. The five extra days I spent with her before trying to reach her aunt by phone again at her place of work went fast. In my mind I suppose I was counting them down. I can't tell you why they flew by. I guess once I knew Rhea existed it all became real to me, Kelsey wouldn't be with me much longer. I believed Eddie's description of his sister was fairly accurate based simply on the sound of her voice. I had little doubt she would be willing to take care of her niece which she had never met, and deep down inside I felt good about that. When she answered the phone, I paused listening to her say, "good afternoon, this is Rhea. How can I help you?"

"Rhea Fallon."

"Yes."

"My name is Sam Pepperell. I'm a detective here in Boston, and I've been doing my best to find you. You have a lovely voice by the way."

"Thank you."

"I have someone that needs your help, and she's quite special. In fact, she came to me special delivery.

"I don't understand. Is this about mom?"

"In a way, your mom is now in an assisted living facility, and she's no longer able to take care of Kelsey. She's the special delivery I mentioned. She's also your only niece."

I could hear some of the emotion I expected erupt through the phone. "She's fine. In fact right now she's down stairs scamming some poor sap out of a dollar using a checkerboard. She started to laugh as she cried. She's

Shannon's daughter and she's seven."

She stammered as she started to ask, "How?"

That's when I told her, "your brother employed me to find you in order to take care of her."

"You know Eddie?"

"Yes. I do. He wants what's best for the kid, and his mom, and I know he thinks the world of you based on our conversations. So, tell me you're willing to help me out on this one."

"Absolutely. Tell her I can't wait to meet her."

"I will. How soon can I expect to see you in Boston?"

"I can be there tomorrow afternoon if that's soon enough. Here, let me get your number."

The call went better than I expected to be honest. It was a lot to lay on someone over the phone, but I had to give her that much of the picture. How she would deal with the situation with her mom, and the fact that her sister was no longer around remained unknown, but Eddie was right about her. She was willing to drop everything, and take on the responsibility handed to her. Sometimes, family tends to bring out the best in people I guess. That's one thing she and Eddie had in common, I suppose.

The next morning I made the trip over to Claudia's place. I was there a little after eight. So, basically, I was on time for once. The kid was enjoying her breakfast which mainly consisted of peanut butter and chocolate covered rice cakes dipped in milk. It wasn't the kind of thing I craved anytime during the day, but Kelsey seemed to like it.

"You're here early," Claudia pointed out.

"Well, I have a surprise for the kid."

Claudia was an all about me kind of woman, and she made that clear as she took a bite out of a strawberry. "What about me?"

"A surprise for you as well." I told her she no longer had to watch Kelsey for me.

"So, you found her."

"Talked to her last night on the phone. She's coming to meet her this afternoon."

"Do you think she'll show?"

"She's her aunt, she has to."

Claudia looked doubtful. "A kid is a big responsibility to just dump on somebody all at once."

"You're telling me." Claudia just gave me her judgmental stare. What? She's her aunt like I said. She has to show up and claim her."

"Yeah, right."

"You do know, not everyone is as jaded as you…" I paused wanting to point the finger at her and leave it there, but she gave me that look forcing me to continue adding, "and me."

Claudia attempted to qualify what I thought about her based on our brief phone conversation. "So, she's not like one of the nut-balls out there, right?"

I looked at her questioning, "who, her Aunt Rhea? No, she seemed like she'd be great for the kid probably exactly what she needs. Why?"

"I'm just trying to make sure you're not sticking her in the hands of some weirdo or something. Believe me there's plenty of them out there." Claudia almost sounded as if she cared about the kid, but she wasn't one for expressing emotion. She preferred to assist others in tapping into theirs.

Whenever we had a difference of opinion we handled it maturely, the way adults do. I'd state where I stood on things, and she'd give me a distinct look right before telling me how she felt about matters. If we couldn't come to terms in a reasonable timeframe, I'd grab my toothbrush before she did something with it I'd regret later, and make a hasty exit before things escalated further. When things really got bad between us I'd just invest in a new toothbrush, and pick my clothes up off her rear stoop when she wasn't there. I had gone through that scenario more than once, often in the dark, and I had learned to look for the boobytraps she planted for me after the first set of stitches were needed near the groin area.

Claudia really knew how to hurt a guy, that's why some of them kept coming back for more. With me, chalk it up to stupidity, maybe it was her assets. She had some big ones. Either way, I figured the crazy part of her cared about me in some way even if she expressed it vengefully at times. Say what you will, it took money and time to string razor wire from the fence, carry it over a puddle, and tie it to a car battery just so I'd get the point. With actions taken like that, there was no doubt she harbored feelings for me, sadistic as they might have been.

It's amazing sometimes what familiar unpredictability will get you into at times. With Claudia, it was usually the emergency room one way or another. I knew all the nurses by first name though, and I never missed a chance to make sure they had my number just in case they had something they wanted me to handle for them, professionally speaking, of course.

Thankfully though, Claudia and the kid had a different relationship which stayed on much better terms than ours.

Chapter 54

Meeting Rhea

My one on one with Rhea centered heavily on what was to come concerning Kelsey's future with her. Rhea was at a point of transition in her life, and I simply figured it might be best for her and the kid if she moved back to Boston. It was just a suggestion, but I made a point of handing her the card of a realtor I knew telling her to make sure she told him I referred her. Then I told her how much Mr. Fuller wanted her back at the accounting firm she used to work for. "The guy sounded sincere. I'd ask for a raise to return there if I were you."

She smiled, it must have given her some reassurance things could turn around for the better at some point. She had a lot on her plate though, and it showed as she said, "you know what they say, you can never truly go back."

Not only did I know the saying, I knew the guy that claimed to be the first to say it. "Fresh starts are often best, I guess, but don't ever forget where you came from." Willard once shared that with me as well. Now, here I was passing those words onto her. That was all I could give as far as advice went which I felt was worth something.

That's when she asked, "do you think people can change?"

Life had taught me a lot of things. We are who we are, and in the end life shapes us into who we become in our own eyes, and the eyes of others. What could I tell her? Life had taught me people for the most part don't change, usually not for the better it seemed, but I was a detective, cynicism was woven into the job description. I wasn't about to tell her Eddie was a lost cause though because I didn't believe that, not anymore. Look who's changing as I speak. Anyway, I told her to keep in mind what Eddie had done for his mother and his niece. I said, "to answer your question honestly, do people change in general, normally I'd say no they don't - not unless they have a good reason to make that change. In Eddie's case he has you, and Kelsey, I say that's more than reason enough, but don't forget he was the one that saw to it Kelsey ended up with you, and not placed in foster care."

"He sure cared. Didn't he?"

"He cared a lot, your brother. Maybe you should go and see him sometime."

"Eddie wouldn't want that."

"I know things don't look good from either side of that glass, but I know he needs you in his life."

"How do you know that?"

"Every man needs something, what's important to Eddie is family." "Well maybe I'll start with a call."

"I know he would like that."

Teddy had done me the favor of hanging out with the kid while I spoke privately with her aunt. I never had to twist his arm to do it either. The two of them spent as much time watching us from a distance as they did conversing with one another. They made quite a pair. Kelsey went to give Teddy his coin back when I took Rhea over to meet her, but the old guy told her, "you keep it. That's yours, something to remember us by."

"I'd listen to him kid. He never parts with money." That brought some levity to the situation. I didn't go so far as to ask if Teddy was feeling alright cause I had a pretty good feeling how he felt at that moment.

Leaving the building, Rhea held Kelsey's hand as she looked down at her saying, "you want to tell Pepper bye, don't you?"

What happened next stays between us, I mean it. If you tell anyone else I'll just deny it because that's the kind of guy I am. The kid did tell me bye, but she never spoke that word out loud. She let go of her aunt's hand, and she walked over to me. That's when she wrapped her arms around me one last time as she said, "thanks for taking care of me Pepper. You're the best detective in the world." I squeezed her a little too tight as I said, "the world is a pretty big place kid." I figured I'd leave her with that, call it what you will.

That's when she said, "you're crushing me."

I loosened my bear-hug saying, "sorry, kid. Guess I don't know my own strength."

That's when the kid had to go and do it. God knows I never expected it. Rhea didn't seem surprised though. She just watched me, and the kid as she wiped a tear away from her cheek. That of course, was when Kelsey kissed mine, then she said, "I love you, Pepper."

I'd tell you I was speechless, but that wasn't quite the case. I managed to say a few words to her before I waved good-bye to her, and her Aunt Rhea. I guess you want to know what those words were don't you. Alright, here they are just one time for the sake of your curiosity. I said in my best tough guy voice, "I love you too kid, always," and I meant it. Words I never shared with a woman somehow came easy on that sidewalk in the heart of Boston. My eyes went a little misty on that one as I let go of her.

As I watched them walk to Rhea's car my mind held only one word in it at that very moment. That word was how. How a sweet little girl like that could take to someone like me, I couldn't explain. Watching them get in the car, I just chalked it up to good fortune on my part and something special on hers. I simply held my hand up returning the wave as I watched them drive away, and that was the end to the most wonderful two weeks in my life.

Before you get all carried away thinking that's because I really loved spending all that time with Kelsey don't forget that, that was also when the Sox beat the Cardinals in the World Series. The curse was finally over, an 86 year span with no championship wins ended that October. So, October 2004 turned out to be the best ever, despite the fact that fall just happens to be the worst time of year for allergies. Sniffle, sniffle...

Chapter 55

What's After Good-bye

Eddie spoke of his niece as being able to break your heart, I blew my nose as I walked back up the steps outside the building where my office was thinking of the kid as my good luck charm. I knew I was going to miss her. I didn't need to be reminded of it, but I had a feeling someone would. I expected Teddy to let me have it as soon as I entered through the front doors, but he didn't. Fact was he was going to miss the kid too, we both were. He had to say something though, you know Teddy. "Well, I guess things worked out alright," he said.

"Yeah, yeah they did."

"I saw her aunt. She seemed nice."

"She was."

"Yeah, that's good. She was kind of pretty too. Wasn't she?"

"What are you getting at?"

"Oh nothing, I just didn't notice any ring on her finger, that's all."

"Teddy."

"What?"

"I know where you're going with this."

"Do you now?"

Teddy turned around walking over to his chair, he started packing up his stuff as he looked at me over his shoulder saying, "I don't know what you're talking about. You probably notice that kind of stuff though being the great detective you are."

Teddy's feathers were ruffled a little at that point, maybe it was his bursitis or perhaps it was something that went deeper than that. Either way I didn't feel I was the cause of it as I snapped back, "what's got you so worked up?"

"Well you sure didn't waste any time finding her."

"It's not like the kid is lost and found property, Teddy. You don't wait thirty days, and if no one claims her she's yours. She was sent to me for a reason, and I found her aunt. That's my job. The kid needs her, not me."

"Ever occur to you maybe she needs you both. I'm just saying, the kid had talent, a little time spent with her and she could be…"

"Don't say it."

"Say what?"

"Whatever you were about to say, I don't want to hear it."

"I know, I'm going to miss her too."

I just nodded my head, no more words needed to be said, but as I turned to walk up the stairs heading toward my office, Teddy felt the need to tell me something else. "Hey you did the right thing, I'm proud of you, and you're right the kid is better off with her aunt than hanging around with you and me."

"Yeah she is."

"Shame though."

"What's that?"

"The kid could have been something special we're talking youngest checker champion ever."

I wasted no time responding with, "yeah. The kid is special, checker champ or not, but you and I will just have to get used to life becoming a little more boring now that she's gone."

"As long as you realize that."

I knew Teddy well, and I knew what he was referring to with his final statement as he picked up his bag, and headed for the door. If you don't know what he was trying to make clear to me you probably don't know Teddy half as well as I think you should. To tell you the truth, I think he just wanted to hear me say it out loud. The kid was special alright, that's why Eddie sent her to me special delivery. Anyway, it was time for me to get back to work. When everyone else called it a day I was still going at it. That just comes with being a P.I. I didn't mind it, work had the ability to take my mind off of other things, like Kelsey for example.

Nearly a week had passed, and I was working another case on a stakeout no less. All was right as it should be. The night was dark, the temp was cold, and I had my car back all to myself, no pestering kid sitting in the front seat beside me. It was quiet except for the passing traffic, and the occasional siren. Yes, Pepper was back in his element once again without his little sidekick asking him endless streams of questions. You'd think that would make a guy like me pretty happy. Wouldn't you? Yeah, I had it made just the way I wanted it, but the quiet may have been a little too quiet for my taste. Alright, it was damn lonely, but I don't want you to think that's why I picked up the phone to call and check-up on Kelsey. It was part of my job, its called case follow-up. In special situations, special cases like hers, I did what was expected of me. So, don't go reading anything into this. Okay?

I held my cell phone to my ear listening to it ring as I watched for any sign of my subject. Rhea answered and I could tell by the sound of her voice she was surprised to hear from me. "Hello."

"Hey, how's it going?"

"Pepper?"

"Yeah it's me. I was just calling to check on the kid, wanted to see how she was doing, you know."

"Oh, I see. Well, everything seems to be going good. She's

brushing her teeth right now as we speak."

"Oh yeah, well that's good. You mind if I speak with her just for a minute?"

"Well, you do know it's after 9:30 right."

"Yeah, so it is. Is it too late to call? I didn't think about the time, I guess I should've."

"Well, it is past her bedtime, but maybe just this once. She loves to talk about you."

"Yeah, well don't believe half of what she says, the kid has a tendency to exaggerate a little."

"Hang on, I'll get her."

I'm sure you've heard that old expression some say at times about something emotional warming your heart. Hearing the kid's voice set my thoughts in motion, and even though it was cool outside, I was warm from head to toe as we spoke on the phone, briefly. The kid even asked about Teddy. Hey, she was only seven, and obviously still not the best judge of character, but don't hold that against her. I'm only kidding, I think. Anyway, I knew it would make Teddy feel good to know the kid still remembered him even though it had only been a week since she had seen him.

Reflecting on Teddy's words I realized what Kelsey needed in her life. She needed someone she and her aunt could depend on, someone who loved them more than anything. They certainly deserved that. I knew exactly who that guy was, and there was nothing he wouldn't do for those he cared about. I ended the call saying, "goodnight kid."

My mind shifted its focus at that point to coming up with a way to deliver what they needed. On the surface it was easier said than done, but isn't everything that way. The problem more often than not is people not doing anything to fix the situation in the first place. Live your life not doing anything to fix problems, and you end up with a whole pile of them, some of which you can't escape. That's when it hit me. I always love it when a plan comes together.

Some would call it a long shot, I'd called it borderline genius coupled with the best chance I had of putting Ernesto Salazar where he belonged, and returning Eddie Fallon to his family. I couldn't reach Eddie at that hour, but I knew where I could find him.

To Be Continued

www.ingramcontent.com/pod-product-compliance
Lightning Source LLC
Chambersburg PA
CBHW070916180626
46817CB00003B/1083